About the author

The love for reading books came to me during my early high school years and then in my later high school years is when I found pure enjoyment in writing. When I write my work comes to life for me; I can see everything unfold right in front of me. If you enjoy writing don't let anything deter you; I promise you won't regret the obstacles of the journey. For me it's not about the destination, but in truth about the journey.

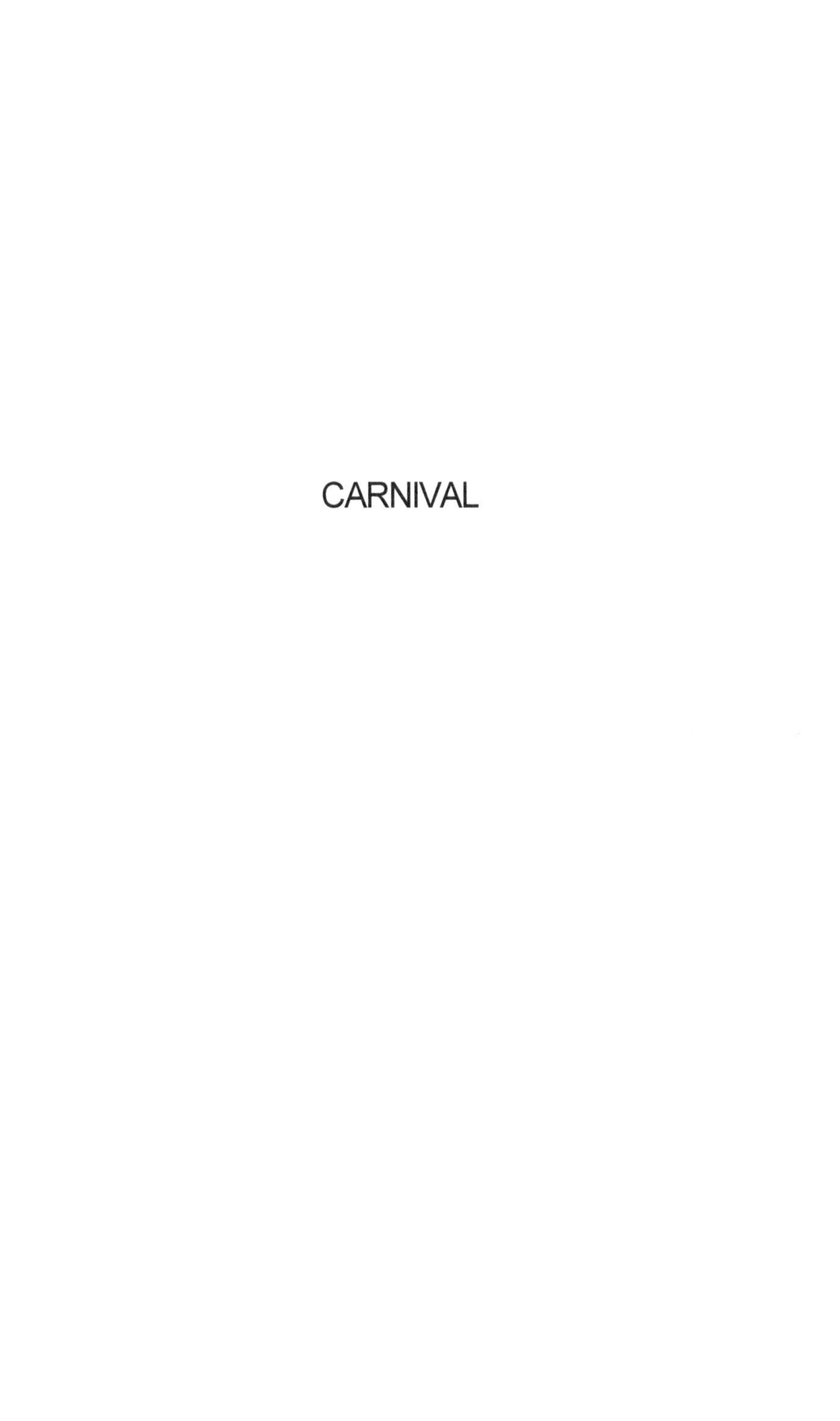

CARNIVAL

Danica Alfter-Maxey

CARNIVAL

Vanguard Press

VANGUARD PAPERBACK

A CIP catalogue record for this title is available from the British Library.

ISBN 978-1-80016-150-4

Vanguard Press is an imprint of Pegasus Elliot MacKenzie Publishers Ltd.
www.pegasuspublishers.com

First Published in 2021

Vanguard Press
Sheraton House Castle Park
Cambridge England

Printed & Bound in Great Britain

Dedication

I’d like to acknowledge my best friend, Rachel Moulton, for bringing my book to life through your drawing. It means the world to me that you’d take time to create this for me.

Written by: Christian Patrick Scully @bean13poetry

It's written on the calendar
Marked in all our diaries
The day and night we love to dread
We call all hallows eve

This year the main spectacular
Is sure to be a scream
The twisted carnival's in town
With sights you won't believe

The acrobats are arsonists
The clowns are killer freaks
A night you're sure never to forget
You may not sleep for weeks

The ring master's a murderer
He leads a killer show
The tent is packed with horrific beasts
Only your nightmares know

With griffins, goblins, ghouls, and geeks
The audience watch enthralled
Some volunteers are plucked out their seats
To clamoring applause

The body count continues to rise
The atmosphere it peaks
When out comes Lord Beelzebub
To name the king of freaks

The winner comes up takes a bow
The tent is all a hush
With one swift strike
Blood soaks the night
And down to hell the audience souls do rush

The devil counts them one by one
The souls of all the dammed
The town can sleep for now it seems
Until the carnival comes back round

Chapter One
The Nightmare

I'm about six years old, I'm still in my pajamas and my bob haircut has major bedhead. Rubbing the left-over sleep from my drowsy eyes, currently I'm not in bed where I should be. I've been taken by some men and being sold to some other men. The exchange is going down in a dark abandoned alley; it's the middle of the night and pouring.

The men are arguing amongst themselves on prices. I can see I'm not the only kid here being cherry picked for the best price. Their voices are menacing and rough and as their voices escalate so does the situation. I hear a bang go off and can only imagine what the noise is, then the guy who originally had me slumped to the ground, not moving, and not talking. With the life fleeing from his eyes, I get thrown into the back of a van without any windows. I see a man sitting on the metal that sits over the back wheel. He's slender with sunken in cheeks and black greasy hair, dressed in a flannel shirt and ratty jeans. As he gives me a sickly smile, he covers my nose and mouth with a cloth. A nasty smell hits my nose and I soon pass out.

When I wake, there is this disgusting taste in my mouth and a chemical smell burned into my nose. Looking around I find that we have arrived to what must be a run-down carnival grounds. As I'm guided into the main tent, I see the most horrifically unimaginable thing in the world. A metal bar structure, expanding at least three-fourths the tent. With kids aging from what looks toddler age to late teens; all malnourished. All extremely sad, with the absence of the childlike spark that most normal kids have.

Some were sitting on the different bars and some laying on pallet made beds, which I assume is where they are all kept when sleeping. Next to each pallet is a few foot chain bolted to the ground with a cuff. Is that to keep them here during the nighttime? A cold chill tingles down my spine. What on earth do they have these kids doing here? And why did they bring me here?

As the days go by and nothing big has happened, I seem to have made one friend. They call her Eighteen; she's super nice and the only one who seems to not have completely given up. Although, sometimes Eighteen scolds me when I don't want to eat what they call food here.

So far, the only peace I get here is when I climb the bars at least four flights up. That's where I am now, and I hear some of the other kids laughing and being carefree. My attention is drawn to them with their sudden happiness. They have these glow sticks, the ones that snap to get them to light up and can make into bracelets. There is this teenage guy, I believe they call him Twenty, a bar below me who gets one thrown up to him and as he pops it, it breaks open. Although when it does, the liquid that spurts from it comes up and lands on my wrist. Burning me like acid or something, but why? Who would put acid in a glow stick? What good would come from that?

Then everything goes black.

I wake up in a trembling sweat, it was a nightmare like no other. Although, that's just the thing, it wasn't a nightmare at all. Was it? No, it had to have been real. I feel like I'm losing my mind over this. I've had this nightmare more times than I can count. With each time experiencing this nightmare, it feels more and more real. With each time something new unraveling, only to bring more questions that I won't get answers to. I need to figure this out if I'm ever going to get any peace. I need to call my parents. As I wait for an answer, I check the clock next to my bed and I see that it's only four thirty in the morning. I need to talk to them though and I won't be able to get back to sleep. It's only after trying my mom for a third time does the call get answered.

"Hey, Mom, I'm sorry for calling at the crack of dawn. Can I come over and talk with you and Dad? It's really important and I don't know how to say it over the phone."

"Of course, darling, I know you wouldn't be up this early if you had a choice. It's a Saturday so anytime you want to come over is fine, and I'll wake your father up now."

"Thank you, Mom, love you."

"Love you too, and see you soon."

After I'm done talking to her; I walk into the bathroom wetting a rag with cold water. Letting it sit on my warm face for a moment then repeating the action one more time. It's only after, that I look at my reflection and it's clear to the naked eye the toll these nightmares are taking on me.

***

It's a short drive from my college dorm to my parents' home. It's currently only five a.m. and all I can think about is the two-way conversation that is bound to happen. While I drive, I play the conversation over and over in my head, trying to find the right words to say. Hating each scenario more than the last. My parents are my adoptive parents. I never wanted them to feel like they weren't good enough, because I wasn't their biological daughter, so I never asked any questions. If I am being completely honest, I never really cared to know. The only real thing that bummed me out was not having any siblings to play with, but even then, I had a ton of cousins that were around my age. I have always been truly content.

It seems like now I might need information on the people who gave me up, and my life before being adopted by my parents. Oh God, I hope they know how much I love them. I just no longer can go without knowing because that nightmare isn't going away. It's only become stronger and more prominent.

As I pull up in front of my childhood home Mom greets me on the porch, a warm smile on her face and a mug of hot chocolate in her hand.

"Where's my cup of hot cocoa?" teasingly I joke. But she is prepared, like she always is when I stop by.

"Right here on the table, darling. Where else?" she lightly laughs. Standing up she greets me with a hug.

"You didn't forget to add cinnamon to it right?" I absolutely love cinnamon in my hot cocoa.

"Of course, who do you think you got the taste for it from?" Mom gasps in fake hurt at my question.

"Where's Daddy?" Sitting I take a small sip of my cocoa.

"Oh, he'll be out in just a minute. He wanted some coffee for himself." She has the slightest wrinkle on the outside of her eyes and permanent smile lines in her cheeks.

As Dad walks out onto the porch, he joins us at the table and squeezes my hand in his. "Hey, Poppie girl, how is college treating you? We haven't heard much from you since this term started a couple weeks ago. Now tell me you are remembering to have a little fun along with all that hard work?"

"Hey, Dad, school is going okay so far. I've got an amazing roommate; we might become friends. But that's not what I came here today to talk to you and Mom about."

"Ah yes, your mom eluded that there might be something heavy weighing on your mind. So, tell us what's going on?"

"So, for you to understand I need to tell you something that I haven't told either of you before. I don't want you to get hurt that I didn't say something before. Can you promise me that you won't get upset?"

"Of course, darling, you can tell your dad and I anything, always." Mom eases me.

"Okay, well I've had this nightmare for as long as I can remember. It's about me when I was six." I tell them every little detail I can remember and as they listen, I can see them studying me. What they don't realize though, is that I'm studying them too. Looking for nonverbal indicators, and boy are they telling me quite a story. One that I don't think I'm going to be so happy with what they have to tell me.

"So now that you know the reoccurring nightmare I have, I need to ask about my biological parents. Who they were, where I lived with them, why they gave me up for adoption. Just everything. I know this sounds totally bonkers, but I feel this nightmare isn't even a nightmare, but real events." Everything I say comes out as rambling, with my words matching the pace of my rapid heartbeat. Only, coming out just above a whisper. During the nerve-racking moments it takes one of them to reply to me I have the urge to bite at my already budded nails. To occupy my hands, I tensely stir my spoon around in my half-drunk cocoa.

"Honey, we adopted you from an agency. It was closed adoption, so there isn't much to tell. And all that came with you was a little light up keychain in the shape of a car. It was purple, and the light in it had already died." Mom places a hand over mine, trying to soothe me. Stopping the motions of the stirring is a futile act though as I'm more upset than before I came over.

"Well how about, did they tell you guys how long I was in foster care before you two came and adopted me?" Desperately, I look between the two of them. My eyes silently pleading with them. Pleading with them to have some information for me.

"Just that you had only been there for a short while, so you didn't have time to understand what was going on. All you knew was that you wanted to go home." Mom doesn't quite look at me but more so looking through me as if she is remembering that time.

"And there isn't anything else? Dad?" I look to him with desperation, I know they are keeping something from me, but I don't understand why. I have a right to know about my past.

"Poppie, I'm sorry but there was nothing more. You didn't even know your own name when we adopted you, so we had to name you ourselves." His voice is husky with guilt barely breeching the surface.

"Oh, okay. Well, I have to go. Um, I just need to be alone for a while. Love you guys." I walk away just barely able to keep the tears at bay until I get into my car and start to drive off.

Why, why won't they tell me? I know they are hiding something; I just don't know what. What could have been so bad that they don't feel they can tell me? This certainly isn't all the information on my past. Surely, I had a family and life before foster care. I mean I was six when I got adopted, dammit!

I need food, and quickly, because I need something to chew on. Damn this fucking anxiety and these nerves. Oh, you know what I'm down for a burger and some fries with a blackberry milkshake.

***

After satisfying my need for food, I go back to my dorm room and try to find any files or paperwork that might have been stored away. Somewhere there needs to be something, anything, that can give me a lead on helpful information. Rummaging through the few boxes I have with me, I realize that I might have more luck at my parents' house but that's an obvious no go.

When I turn up empty handed, I come up with the greatest idea ever and don't know why I didn't think of this before…

Maybe, if I check with the foster care I was adopted from, they must at least know the name of my biological mom and maybe even Dad. That's a starting place at least. I do have my adoption papers that have the name of the foster care. It's also one of the only documents I talked my parents into giving me when I was younger.

I call the foster care, but I have no luck. All I get is their voicemail telling me their office hours. I guess I will have to pay them a visit when their office hours are open. With growing excitement coursing through my veins at the possibility of learning about my past, I can't wait for the morning to head out on this journey. I know for a fact I won't be getting anything close to the ten hours minimum of sleep that my body demands.

Chapter Two
Poppie's Journey

New Journey's is what it is called, that much I remembered on my own, so I didn't need to ask my parents. They don't know that I called New Journey's the other day or that I'm headed there now. After looking up its location I find that it's a couple states away from me, in Kirby, Wyoming. That means I have to ditch school for a couple days. Shit, I really shouldn't be skipping, but I don't really have any other choice. The good thing is I only have to worry about missing school, not school and work.

My parents are executives at my Uncle Bill's law firm; one being an executive administrative assistant to and the other being an executive personal secretary. We've lived a pretty well-off life, though I do have to give credence where it is due, both my parents are extremely hard workers.

I struck a deal with my parents and my Uncle Bill, that if I work as a receptionist at his law firm during the summertime, I don't need to have one while I focus on school. It was all their idea, but I'm grateful they would do this for me, so I can solely focus on school. Between what I save up during the summer and the 'allowance' my parents give me each month I don't have to worry about money at all during school.

It's eight a.m., my bag is packed and I'm ready to go. It's a fourteen-hour drive, and that's without any stops. Dammit I won't be able to talk to anyone today, they'll be closed by the time I roll in. Still giddy at what I am about to do, all I need to do now is crank up the music and settle in for the ride.

***

I roll up to a Motel 6, I've made the drive in twelve hours and forty-five minutes, it's eight forty-five p.m. I may or may not have broken a few speeding laws. I really hope they have a vacancy; I am so damned tired, and hungry. Once I get settled in my room I decide to call and get Chinese food delivered to my room. They said it's about half an hour until it'll be here, and I need a shower to get the drive off me.

'Knock, knock, knock' "A.B.A Chinese." I hear a muffled voice and walk to the door.

"That'll be $14.95 and delivery is $5 so your total is $19.95."

"All righty, here is $25, the rest you can have as a tip. Thank you." I close the door behind him. Orange chicken and chow mein with some egg rolls and pot stickers on the side. All my favorites! Yum! Time to dig in, and then turn in for the night.

As I flip through channels on the TV, nothing catches my eye, then I flip to the ION channel. The show is reruns of *Criminal Minds*, I used to love that show right after being adopted, but I haven't watched it in years. The familiarity of the love interest between Garcia and Morgan and the intelligence of Reid. It brings a pang in my heart for a simpler time when I finally felt safe and loved. Now watching it, I see it from an adult view and the comfort is renewed. Once I get everything figured out, I think I'll purchase the series and binge watch them.

Right as I'm about to fall asleep my phone rings; I've been ignoring my parents' calls all day. As I look at the caller I.D., my face lights up, it's Jeremy my boyfriend of going on two years.

"Hey, babe, where are you? I haven't heard from or spoken to you all day and Bridget said she hasn't seen you since Friday."

"Jer, I need to tell you something really important, but I need you to promise not to freak. Okay? Promise."

"Poppie? What's going on?"

"You have to promise me first."

"Of course, I promise."

"Okay, so I'm in a different state right now, it was an impulse thing. But a needed thing as well. Tomorrow I'm going to the foster care I was in before I got adopted by my parents; I need to find out about the people who gave me up."

"Poppie, where are you exactly?"

"I'm in Kirby, Wyoming. Hear me out though, I've had this reoccurring nightmare for as long as I can remember, and the dream is so vivid and real that I think it has something to do with my past. I talked with my parents and they couldn't give me any information that could help me. I need to figure this out, it's driving me nuts, which brings me here. I will be back in just a day or so, and I will keep safe. Oh, and if my parents get ahold of you please don't tell them what I'm doing. I think they are hiding something from me and I'm not ready to simply let this go."

"I will only agree to that if you call me every day. I've never seen you this determined to find these people and I don't want you to have to go through this all alone. Do we have a deal?"

"I can work with that, babe. I love you, Jer."

"I love you too, Poppie, sleep tight. Oh, and one other thing I know this is important to you but no matter what happens I'll always be here, who your parents are and what your life was before you were adopted won't ever change how I feel about you. You know unless they're apart of the mafia and try to kill me, then of course you're on your own."

"Gee, thanks, asshole."

"You know I'm only screwing with you. Bye, babe." His laughter makes me smile.

"Bye, babe."

I turn off the TV and let myself naturally doze off to sleep.

***

It's eight a.m. and I use my car's gps to direct me to New Journey's; it's about two miles from the motel I'm staying in and with every minute that passes by my nerves start eating away at me. I don't know what I should expect from this, maybe I should go home and forget about this whole damned thing. That's when I receive a text from Jeremy and I have Siri read the text to me, so I can be hands free and not get distracted or pulled over.

Siri- "Jeremy says"- "I love you and I am so proud of you. You've got this, Poppie."

With renewed strength I pull into New Journey's parking lot. As I walk up to the door, I take a deep breath and enter the building. Following the signs to the office is simple enough, the door is open, and I can see a woman sitting behind a desk. Her desk name plate reading, Judith.

"Excuse me, Judith."

"Yes, how may I help you?"

"I was a foster kid here when I was about six, and well I need to know about the people who gave me up and where I came from. I mean that's the best way I can describe it. I have my adoptive papers, the birth certificate that was given to my adoptive parents and I have my driver's license. I also have my social security card if you need it. Please I need to know."

"Okay, let me take these for a moment and see what I can find for you. You actually came really prepared for this, most people don't. If you'll just take a seat right over there, I'll, call you back over once I've found something." She gestures to the waiting area in the office. Taking a seat, I slump down, a huge weight washes over me as my mind starts to wander again. *Shit, Poppie you want to know. You will never get anywhere in life if you flee away from a complex situation.* I need to pull myself together.

"Miss Poppie. I'm ready for you now."

"What did you find?"

"Well, frankly not much was ever filed with us. It gives us your date of birth, which is still the same one you go by today, but to dig deeper you need a court order to unseal your history. Unfortunately, I can't even look in it to give you any information either. All it says is that to unseal the file you need to go to the courthouse in Angel Fire, New Mexico."

"Hold on, let me get a pen and paper out. Okay, so you said, Angel Fire, New Mexico?"

"That's correct, and here are some papers you'll need to present to the judge along with the papers you brought today."

"Um, is there a time limit on this? You see I'm currently attending Kansas State University, and so I can't take too many days off in a row and by the time I get home I will have already missed a day or two.

Honestly, I hate even missing one, there is so much you can miss in a day."

"Don't I know it. Even in my day missing a day could set you back a few days on your course load. There is no expiration date for this document. Just don't lose it or you'll have to go through the awful system to get another copy."

"Thank you so much for your help today, Judith. Um, one more thing though, can I have a copy of my file. I don't know if my adoptive parents got one when they adopted me, but I'd really be happy if I could have one of my own."

"I think I can work that just give me a couple minutes to get copies made." As she walks away into a restricted part of the office I patiently wait. I haven't found what I'm looking for yet, but I'm at least one step closer. Now more than ever, the fire burns deep to find out more about my past. Only now it has become a reality no longer an idea. As she hands me a file, I graciously thank her and head my way back to the motel.

After checking out I stop at a convenience store gas station, filling up my tank and grabbing a soda and some snacks. While there I decide to call Jeremy. "Hey, Jer, so I've got a little bit of a lead. Nothing to exciting, but a step closer."

"That's awesome, babe. So, where to now?"

"For now, home. I don't want to miss more school than absolutely necessary, and I need a little time to process the information I got. I should be home no later than noon tomorrow. I want you to come over to my dorm if you would?"

"Do you even need to ask. Of course, babe. Just let me know when you get into town and I can be at your dorm to greet you."

"That would make you the best boyfriend in the world. Jeremy, I'm serious, if you come over and just let me vent about every little detail. There would be nothing better."

"Wear pajamas and drink hot cocoa."

"You treat me too good; you know that."

"I'll see you tomorrow, Poppie."

"See you tomorrow, Jer."

Entering the highway, I'm just barely at the beginning of my journey home. Knowing that in less than twenty-four hours I'll be home, with Jeremy at my door waiting for me it's hard to keep to the posted speed limit.

Chapter Three
Home

It's midnight Tuesday morning, though to me it's still Monday considering I haven't been to sleep yet. My eyes are dry from staring at the road for so long in the last twenty-four hours. With my bag strapped over my shoulder I approach my dorm room door. I'm skimming over my file and bump into Jeremy. I had called him about an hour ago letting him know how far out I was.

"Hey, babe," brightly he says with a small smile on his face. I lean into him and hug him tightly. I've never missed someone so much in such a short amount of time.

Jeremy knows everything about me, about a year ago, we were a year into our relationship. I decided to spill everything to him, everything that is except my reoccurring nightmare. Until now I never had the desire to dig into my past. It was never important to me who gave me life, what mattered was that the people who adopted me actually wanted me and never failed to show that they loved me.

"Jer! Oh, I'm so happy to see you! Um, I feel really bad for saying this, but I'm so bloody exhausted from all the driving and am having a really hard time keeping my eyes open. I've been so excited to see you all day and now all I can think about is my bed."

"Let's go sleep for a while then."

"Are you sure? I can probably stay up for a little while longer, I feel so bad that I had you come over and now all I can think about is sleep."

"I'm sure. Come on, my little walking zombie."

As I get into bed Jeremy lays next to me while I nod off. The warmth of his body is completely welcoming.

In a blink of an eye I am woken up by an unforgiving ray of sunlight. I don't know what time it is, but Jeremy is no longer lying next to me. I hear his voice in the living room. He must be talking to my roommate Camille.

"Hey, sleepy head, you were out for a good ten hours or so, it's already ten thirty a.m. Camille woke up not too long ago, and we've just been chit chatting, waiting for you to get up."

"That's my cue to leave, I just didn't want him to feel awkward with me here not saying anything to him and you sleeping."

"You're more than welcome to hang out with us, right, Jer?"

"Yah, Camille, you're more than welcome to hang out with us."

"Actually, my schedule is pretty busy today, but can I get a rain check. I'd really like to be friends with you guys."

"Okay, but I'm going to hold you to it even if it's just us girls. I'm in need of another girl best friend. Jer is a great boyfriend and best friend, but he doesn't do all the girly things. And a girl can never have too many gal pals."

As Camille heads out the door to wherever her next destination, I plop down next to Jeremy on the couch and give him a chaste kiss on the lips.

I've decided I won't go to classes today, but I'll be back in them tomorrow. Thankfully, that means I'll only have missed two days of school.

"How was your sleep?"

"Sleep? It felt like my body was dead weight. I'm surprised I even made it to my bed. I'd say it was more of a mini coma." He hugs me, and I lean all my weight into him.

"So, when are you going to tell me what you found in Wyoming?"

"Well the lady I talked with, Judith, she gave me my file. Though, when she tried to dig deeper, she got blocked by a sealed file. Judith told me that I would have to go to the Angel Fire, New Mexico courthouse to make an appeal to get my file unsealed. I just don't know when I'll be able to take that kind of time off. I might have to wait until summer break to manage that amount of time. And if I just tell my uncle that it's a fun road trip you and I are going on, then he won't care at all. Which brings me to you, would you go with me? I know it might take a week or two to get it all processed, but at least we would be together on an adventure."

"Of course, I will just have to request the time off at work. Since it is already May 8th, I'll need to put in for the time off tomorrow when I am at work. Can I see what's in your file?"

"Oh shit, I'm sorry, of course you can."

As midday turns into late night, we binge watch *Criminal Minds*. I talked Jeremy into taking my debit card and buying the first two complete seasons. He's never heard of or seen *Criminal Minds*, but as I hoped, he became an instant fan. And even in one of those cute stubborn ways, got mad at me for having to pause when I had to get up.

On the couch, curled up in blankets, with all my weight against him. As he is softly stroking my hair, I felt my eyelids get heavy over my eyes. Not long after, I am sound asleep, in pure bliss.

Like all good things, my blissful slumber doesn't last long. I wake up in a panic, the vivid memory of the pain caused by the acid glow stick. There is no actual pain on my wrist nor is there a mark from it. I hope when I get this all figured out, the nightmare will go away. As I look over at Jeremy, he is so peacefully sleeping, but then again, he most definitely could easily sleep through a tornado. Or better yet, on a more humorous side, a woman in labor. I don't want to wake him, but that is an awfully uncomfortable looking sleeping position.

“Jer… babe?” His body twitches as trying to recognize the source of noise. The familiarity of the voice calling to him. “Babe, let’s go to bed. Put your arms around me and I’ll guide you in, you don’t even have to fully wake up,” I whisper.

“Mmhmm… where you will take advantage of me.” I think he is more asleep than awake, and it is sweet, and extremely attractive that he wants me even in his dreams.

“Oh yes, but first, sleep.” I quietly laugh. As I stand him up, I turn my back to him and place his hands on my shoulders. Slowly walking to my room. Gently plopping him on my bed it’s hard not to stare at the smoothed features on his face. Deep set eyes, slender nose; eyebrows bold but not thick and a mouth that even in its resting state is slightly uneven. I could go on, but best described… Perfect.

***

With the hours passing and approaching the wee hours of the morning, I can’t sleep a wink. My mind won’t shut off, I’m getting restless and irritated. As my thoughts consume me, I think back on Angel Fire, New Mexico. Why can’t I simply go to any courthouse in the country and get the information I need. Everything is connected through the states when it comes to adoption cases, especially now with the internet.

My only logical thought is to do research on Angel Fire, New Mexico, and its courthouse.

Chapter Four
And So Begins the Road Trip

It's been a month or so since I got back from Wyoming, and yesterday was the last day of the term. Today, Jeremy and I leave for Angel Fire, New Mexico. From my home here in Lawrence, Kansas to Angel Fire, New Mexico is about a ten-hour drive. Our day is starting at eight a.m. should put us there by dinner time.

"Angel Fire or bust?" Squeezing my hand Jeremy looks at me.

"Angel Fire or bust!" I squeeze his hand back and we get into his Jeep. The first ever trip Jeremy and I have taken together.

"To our first of many adventures." I lean over and quickly take a picture of us to document this for us both. His goofy self, he smiles and poses for the picture.

***

Driving through Kansas is a breeze, with the conversation never ending, plenty of snacks and our favorite drinks from Starbucks.

As we get to the border of Oklahoma, I have Jeremy pull over and have him take a picture with me in front of the state sign, breathing in the fresh air. The sign for Tyrone, the closest city is in eyesight of the border. It's about one thirty, so we will most likely stop there for lunch and stretch our legs.

The shoulder of the highway is enough for us to safely park, but the gust of wind from a diesel truck is so strong that I need to steady myself to not blow away. Jeremy laughs at me having to brace myself against him.

"Thanks for that. I thought I was going to blow away when that truck passed us. Let's get going again. I hope that the motel we stay at has a pool; I could go for a good swim right about now, I even packed my swimsuit in case."

"Oh well, looks like great minds think alike, I've packed my swim trunks as well, so I can swim with you."

Climbing back into his Jeep he looks over and winks at me with a devious smile. Damn I love how he makes me feel desired. Wanted with that primal instinct, but especially with him I've never felt like an object. It's so much more than that with Jeremy.

"Hey, babe, can we stop over in Tyrone and get some food? I'm starving." Wrapping my arms around his arm that is lazily placed on the shifting stick, I lean on him lightly.

"Food does sound really good right about now. I hope they have a good burger joint in town." He leans down to quickly kiss the top of my head, then looks back at the road.

"Yes! I hope they have milkshakes too. A blackberry milkshake and fries sound scrumptious!" I hum at the thought of such delicious food.

***

We had seriously lucked out; Tyrone had a Sonic!

No way are your chili cheese tots better than my blackberry milkshake and fries," I challenge sticking with my milkshake.

"You wanna bet, how about tonight's dinner? Winner chooses and loser pays." Jeremy cockily smirks and puts his hand out to make the bet.

"Oh, you are so on, buster!"

After we shake hands and trade food for a moment…

Turns out he lost, but at a cost to me. The chili didn't sit well on my stomach. Nicely put, I was bowing to the porcelain throne in the Sonic's bathroom for a good ten minutes before I felt settled enough to move. Walking out of the bathroom after rinsing out my mouth, smiling and laughing at Jeremy's expression.

"Solid bet, Jer, now I'm going to enjoy my blackberry milkshake and buy more fries that aren't stone cold."

"So not funny, Poppie. How are you feeling? You sure you're good to eat anything else?" His face is in that stubborn upset look, which causes me to laugh even more.

"I feel good, plus I just won the bet, loser!" I put an 'L' on my forehead at him.

After we gorged ourselves with bomb food, we again stretched our legs for a couple minutes then got back on the road. As we drive these long hours everything starts to blend in together. At one point in our drive from Tyrone we had to take an exit off the highway we've been on to this point. To follow the directions the GPS has given us we got directed to an old country highway similar to route 66 but I didn't catch the name of it. I smile to myself as I listen to Jeremy go between singing and humming along to the songs that play on the radio. Jeremy is an extremely talented singer, though on some songs he purposefully sings off-key. Without even trying he makes me smile and my heart beat fast. He's the sweet levelheaded one to my wild and sassy. He met me during one of my wild sassy moments and hasn't left my side yet. Of course neither one of us was looking for anything more than friendship at the time; we had about six months of being friends before we started dating.

It was junior year when we met, it was at a New Year's party thrown by Toby, Bridget's boyfriend. The party was so chaotic, with people and empty bottles everywhere. I had already had too much to drink and so Bridge and Toby had me go in Toby's room to pass out and stay safe. But me being me, I had other plans. With the bedroom door closed and the loud music still booming clear through the walls, I feel wild and carefree. Stripping down to my underwear and bra, my hair down I dance. Losing myself in the moment, I don't hear him at first. Lowly he laughs, then I see him. This charismatic looking teen boy was there grabbing a blanket off the bed to cover me with. I hadn't met him before, but I knew who he was, Jeremy Ross. He was a baseball player but wasn't like other jocks with an ego that makes you just want to punch them. Not to say he wasn't popular, he just wasn't flashy or a dick.

In that moment all he was worried about was covering me up. Then the next thing I knew I was waking up in Toby's room with a guy over in the corner asleep in a chair, arms folded across his chest, with his torso leaning against the back of the chair, head leaning all the way back and his lips slightly parted.

"Um... Hello?" Raspy, my throat raw and my head pounding I gently rub my hand on his arm to wake him up.

"Huh... What?" Unfolding his arms, he rubs his eyes with the base of his palms.

"Not to be rude but do you know how I got to be in my underwear?" I clutch the blanket around my entire body. I whisper as to not give myself a headache.

"All I know is that I came in here to get away from my ex who was being a total bitch and I couldn't in my right mind leave you vulnerable like that." He clears his throat, standing he stretches.

"Did I do anything, um... did I make any sexual advances towards you? When I get drunk like that, I sort

of do wild things." Dropping the blanket, I get back into my clothes. Jeremy blushes slightly and looks away. It's cute how modest he is being.

"Nothing wild besides what I already mentioned. But you looked cute how you were dancing. Perfectly content with being you, even if that was drunk you. I'm Jeremy by the way." He puts his hand out for me to shake, putting my hand in his I feel his warmth.

"I'm Poppie. I've seen you around before, you're a really good baseball player. Oh, and sorry you had to play babysitter to me. I do get damn wild when I drink, you should have seen me last time. It was again at one of Toby's parties and well first I started out the night with strip poker, then Toby, Bridge, and I with a few other people I don't remember their names. We went and broke into the water park we have here. Needless to say, there were empty bottles everywhere and despite the water being freezing I couldn't feel it. When we got caught, I took full responsibility, you know because it was my idea. They banned me until I'm twenty-one and I had to clean the place up and got to A.A. meetings until the judge cleared me. Which was only once a week for a month. I think they just wanted to see that I went and took responsibility for my reckless behavior." I laugh, no shame here.

"Damn, I might have to tag along with you sometime to see that side of you. Maybe make sure you don't get yourself into too much trouble." Jeremy smirks at me.

"More the merrier, although I'm pretty down to earth and kind of boring when I'm sober. So, you gotta be willing to hang with both, because once you're a part of the group I hang out with there is no way out. So, knowing what you know now, are you still sure you want to?" I give him a devious smile arching one of my eyebrows.

"I don't know you, but I have a strong feeling there isn't a boring bone in your body." He looks sincere. In a split moment without thinking I kiss him once and then walk out of the room to get something non-lethal to drink, leaving a dumbfounded Jeremy in the bedroom. Although, he quickly regains his faculties and follows out behind me.

I stop in the living room to look around for a moment at the damage done. While walking through to the kitchen I see that Bridge and Toby are already awake and chatting amongst themselves. I hear Jeremy behind me.

"Hey, what was that kiss for..." Jeremy stops in his tracks as he sees them.

"Naughty girl. You kissed Jeremy?" She gives me a huge grin.

"Yah, he was nice. You were nice, and I wanted to. But don't worry I don't expect anything, I don't want a relationship right now. And if memory serves me correctly, from what you said a few minutes ago. I vaguely remember you saying something about dodging

an ex-girlfriend last night." I give him my best innocent look.

"You're right I did say that. I'm not really looking to be in a relationship right now. I just need to be me for a while." He almost stares me down at how intently he looks at me.

"Hey if you guys are done with this love fest, Bridge and I were going to go to Denny's to get some food. You want to join us?" Toby smirks, then him and Bridge bump fists at his smartass remark.

"Love you guys too," I stick out my tongue to them, "but yes I'm down, and we aren't really going to give Jeremy a choice, right? He's one of us now. I told him if he's down to be my friend he has to be all in." I grab his hand and head out to Toby's car with Toby and Bridge right behind us.

Eating breakfast at IHOP we talk and laugh. Mainly all of them laughing at me from what I tell them I did last night instead of passing out when Toby left.

"You're hopeless, Pop." Bridge tosses a piece of bacon at me.

"Pop?" Jeremy asks.

"It's her nickname Bridge here gave her. What when you guys were eight?" Toby lets Jeremy in on the goofy nickname.

"Yup, lifers, Bridge and Pop." Not letting the piece of bacon go to waste I show it off to Bridge and then eat it. "Guys, you know me, I was bound to do something impulsive. Anyways life would be terribly boring

without me." Taking a bite of food, I give them a closed mouth grin that stretches from ear to ear.

"Hey I wanna know something. How long have you two been friends?" I look between Jeremy and Toby.

"Freshman year, right, Toby?" Jeremy confirms with Toby.

"Yup, we were both trying out for basketball and Jeremy here got me in the head with a ball. Been friends since." Toby laughs.

***

Soon I come back out of my reminiscing. I don't know how long I have been in my own thoughts or where we are, but it is dusk out, though, there is still a considerable amount of cars on the highway.

"Hey, Jer, where are we and what time is it?" I look over at him.

"Hey, welcome back, Poppie. Where'd you go in your thoughts? Oh and it's almost seven. I checked GPS and according to it we are about five miles from our exit for where our motel is." He yawns.

"Oh, babe, you should have let me know you were getting tired. I would have taken over the wheel. You made great time though, Jer. Taking into consideration the time we took during our stops; we didn't do too bad." I do a full body stretch. Feeling the deep compression of my back muscles on my spine, followed by the sweet release of the tension that set in while I was lost in the memory.

"I'm all right, my eyes are just a little dry. Anyways, you were so lost in thought I didn't want to disturb you. It must have been something nice though, your face was stuck in a smile the entire time." Briefly he looks over and smiles at me. I softly bring my hands up and touch my cheeks. I can feel the slight ache in my cheeks from all the smiling.

"It was, I was remembering back to when we first met at Toby's party and the morning after when we went for food." I bring his hands to my lips, taking a moment to breathe in his scent then I softly kiss his hand.

Chapter 5
Angel Fire

We pull up to a small locally owned motel in Angel Fire, New Mexico. “Jer, you go in and get us a room, I will grab our bags.” I smile at him.

“No, I got the bags, you don’t have to worry about it.” Painfully he stretches, and sheepishly smiles at me.

“Jer, let me do this. I can see your body is tense from the long hours. I got this.” I get up on my tiptoes and kiss him on the cheek.

“Thanks, babe.” He squeezes my hand and walks into the check in desk in the lobby.

As we make it up to our room on the second floor, there isn’t anything special about the room. It has a king-sized bed, a bathroom with a standing shower, and a dresser for if you so desire to use it. As well, there is a small square table with two chairs and a mini fridge. Nothing fancy, but it will do the job for us. An added bonus, Jeremy made sure to ask for a room that is a non-smoking one, so it doesn’t have that stale stench of cigarettes. I absolutely loath smoking, I tried one once when I went to my first party freshman year and almost threw up. It had a terrible taste, smell, and what it did to my lungs was awful. The really great thing is Jeremy doesn't smoke either and thank God he doesn't because I would not be able to kiss him. Don't get me wrong, I mean that in the nicest way possible. Just the thought of kissing someone who smokes makes me gag.

Jeremy plops down on the bed bouncing a couple times. I laugh at the silly face he is making at me, being totally goofy.

"Hey, babe, do you want me to go out and get you anything. You drove the entire way here and I feel bad that I wasn't the chattiest company." Standing there I feel budding tears on the brim of my eyes, but I wipe them away before he can see them. Although, seemingly enough he saw them before I had the chance.

"Oh, Poppie, I'm okay, really." Standing, he pulls me into a warm hug and soothes me. "What's going on, babe?"

I fight with myself because I know exactly what I'm feeling. My only problem is putting my feelings into words and hoping that Jeremy understands. I hate this why do I have to feel this way now, of all the damned times I could have had these doubts. Now the tears freely flow unchecked. I need to sit down; I walk away from his embrace and sit on the floor with my back against the wall and knees pulled to my chest. Breathing in deeply, letting the air compress in my lungs, slowly letting the air back out and repeating that again a couple more times. Sitting down next to me Jeremy pulls me to his side and wraps his arms around me, not saying anything.

"Get my mind off my own damned thoughts. No scratch that, I need a drink. I don't want to get drunk. I just want either two shots or a beer, I'm not sure which yet. I wonder if this mini fridge has those tiny liquor bottles." I get up and check the fridge, no such luck. "I think God is trying to tell me something here. No alcohol, and I didn't think to bring my fake I.D."

"Maybe just take another moment and breathe. I'm not even as cool as you, I don't own a fake I.D." Jeremy jokes with me; what's even funnier is that I already know he doesn't have one. That brings an undeniable grin to my face. "Ah! I got you to smile!" Smiling, I stand up and stick my tongue out at him. Mood being lifted, I laugh. It is the kind of laugh that comes from the gut and has you grabbing your sides with happy tears coming from your eyes.

"I'm having these debating thoughts with myself on if this is actually the right thing to do. I mean there are a good number of outcomes that are not in my favor. What if I find my parents and they are horrible people? What happens if my parents are dead and all I get are their grave sites? Or… Or what if they never wanted me to begin with? I don't remember anything from before I got adopted. Maybe I can't mentally bear the answers given. I don't think I can do it, Jer." Rambling I start to hyperventilate, I need to cool down. Walking into the bathroom, quickly grabbing a wash rag, and wetting it, I apply the cool rag to the back of my neck and another one to my face.

"I-I-I'm sorry, I'm letting fear cloud my desire to know. If I don't try to find answers, I might never get rid of the nightmare. Jer, thank you for coming with me." I can feel my heart rate go back to normal.

"Of course, I even would have come with you last time if I knew you were going." He soothes and hands me some snacks to munch on. I lightly chuckle in my mind; he knows that with my anxiety I have worked up a nervous appetite.

The rest of the night, Jer talked with me about fun goofy things until I passed out.

***

It's eight a.m., digging through a small backpack to find the notepad that had the date, time, and address of my meeting with Judge Rowan. According to my notepad, it's today obviously, at ten a.m. in his office.

"Poppie, how about we go for a quick swim in the pool before the meeting? Have a little fun before all the seriousness?" Wiggling his eyebrows at me, it's an offer I can't refuse.

"Hells yah! Only for forty-five minutes to an hour though. I want to be at least five minutes early." We change quickly grabbing towels, we're out the door and at the pool within minutes.

***

As we wait outside Judge Rowan's office to be called in, I keep a firm grip on Jeremy's hand. Watching as whom I can only assume are city officials mill around doing their jobs only eats at my nerves more. I can feel his thumb making a smooth circling motion, something that helps keep both of our nerves at bay.

"Miss Poppie Raven, I'm ready for you now." The judge opens his door and peeks out at us.

"Hi, Judge Rowan, this is my boyfriend, Jeremy Ross. Would it be all right if he came in with me?" Judge Rowan shakes my hand and then Jeremy's.

"That is up for you to decide if you want Mr. Ross to be present. I do not mind either way." He leads us into his office and directs us to sit down in the two chairs opposite his desk. The chairs are the diamond back padded leather kind with the metal brads that outline the front of the arms of the chair running down to the wooden legs of the chair. The kind you would find in an attorney's office. His office also has the slight hint of what can only be a cigar that must have been puffed on recently.

"Along with talking to you I also received a call from Mrs. Judith Malroy from New Journey's. She seemed really anxious to help in any way she could. Did you remember to bring your file and two forms of legal identification?" He looks up from some papers on his desk.

"Yes, your honor, I did. Although, will it be a problem if the names don't match from when I entered into foster care? Because my parents that adopted me said that foster care had no idea what my name was before I came to them and so my adoptive parents renamed me." I hand over all the paperwork I have and my forms of identification.

I set the small backpack that was draped over my shoulders on the floor. Looking at Judge Rowan, he is a slender man with salt and pepper hair and has the faint smell of aftershave. We sit in silence for a good fifteen minutes while Judge Rowan studiously went over the paperwork on his desk and some other information on his computer. I feel myself stealing glances Jeremy's way, more than I'd like to admit, while waiting for Judge Rowan to say something to us. I can hear the ticking of his grandfather clock and I start to bite at my nails of the hand that Jeremy isn't holding, but I know to be patient and to wait for him to speak first. He sighs, stopping to take a drink from his glass of water. Placing his fingers to his temples to release stress building up, he looks up at us for the first time since I handed him my paperwork.

"Looking thoroughly through your paper files and the files we have of you on in our system. I must say that you might not like what you hear, but I won't hold anything back from you. Now, before I disclose this information, Miss Raven, are you sure you don't want me to privately tell you this and then you can decide what to share with Mr. Ross?" My stare doesn't falter with the judge and neither does my grip on Jeremy's hand.

"I want him here with me, there's no one I trust more than this guy right here." Jeremy squeezes my hand lightly in response to what I've said. It makes my heart flutter ever so slightly.

"Before I start, I would like to mention that there is also the option for you to take this file I have here, it's a copy of your entire file and read it through privately. Of course, I already know what's in here, but you don't have to go through the awkward feelings of hearing it all from a stranger. If you do decide to take it with you to privately go over the information, just know I'm not leaving anything out. What we have on you in our files is all we have." He sits quietly while I think over my options for a moment. The generosity of his offer catches me off guard for a brief moment.

"That would be great actually, give me time to process everything without having to keep my composure." Tension I didn't know I had releases from my body.

"How much do I owe for this visit and the copy of my records?" I ask as I put the file into my backpack.

"Here, take this slip of paper down to the court clerk, that's where you'll pay. It'll be about a $100 give or take, but I'm rooting for you so I'm going to make a note on here to get you a little discount." Quickly he scribbles something and then wishes me luck.

***

It's been an hour after we thanked Judge Rowan and made our gracious departure from the courthouse, the file has been left unopened on the motel room table. *Fucking shit.* Knowing I hold the only logged information on my past, I've lost my damn nerve. All I can think about is eating to appease my anxious thoughts. Quickly, I look in the drawer of the nightstand and find the Yellow Pages book to look up restaurants in this town. Yellow Pages are basically obsolete at this point, but I figure why not see if there are any locally owned establishments.

"Okay, how about this, let's go for lunch and then come back and open the file? And I mean a complete get away from this motel, eating at the fast-food joint. Knowing that you've been fed to help calm you would make me feel like I'm actually able to help you." He grabs my hand before I can answer or find a good place to eat, is leading me out to his car.

"Wait! We don't know where we are going yet, Jer?" exasperated, I let him pull me out to the car.

"Live a little, babe! We'll drive and whatever place we pass first, that we actually like, we'll stop at." Laughing he opens my door then goes to the driver's side to get in. His carefree adventure side is almost the mirror image of mine. Almost, being the key word there. The thought brings a silent laugh to my mind.

"All right, but you know I'm a serious foodie and wherever we go better have a buffet style line up." Mumbling I buckle up for this mini adventure.

My heavy heart doesn't go away, if anything I have an even more ominous feeling in my heart and gut. It's not long before I zone out, leaving this present world for a semblance of an alternate reality. A reality that is more of a nightmare than anything else.

"Twenty-seven, don't do that! You need to eat." Eighteen yells at me. I've pushed away my tray of 'food' that my captors have given me. It's not the first time I've done this, the food is grey like an expired gravy and along with that stale bread that has mold growing on it and water that would need to be purified at least a dozen times to be FDA approved. This 'stuff' makes me sick, literally. How can they expect us to eat this? Are they trying to kill us? I just really want to go home; I'm forgetting my family and what they look like. I can't even for the life of me remember my own name. There are so many of us that they just give us numbers. Eighteen told me that it also helps them keep track of us and makes it easy for prospective buyers. Eighteen is the only one who is actually nice to me. She watches out for me; she's been here so long that these people are all she knows.

"Twenty-seven, they'll see you and you know what will happen. I don't want it to happen to you again, please just eat at least the bread. All you need to do is scrap off the bits of mold and here put this piece of cloth

over the mouth of the cup, it will filter the water some when you drink it." Scooting closer to me she shows me little things to make the food a smidge better.

"Thank you, Eighteen. Eighteen, when do I get to go home? When do you get to go home?" I plug my nose while taking a bite of the bread. It's so stale I can't believe I haven't broken a tooth from it. Eighteen has a sad broken emotion flash across her face, but it's quickly replaced with quiet determination.

"I'm sorry, Twenty-seven, but we don't get to go home. Unfortunately, we are here to stay. How about this, Twenty-seven. I'll be your sister and you can be mine; we will at least have each other. How does that sound?" Her smile is half-hearted and with sadness in her eyes.

Whipping my head to the sound of a car horn, bringing me back to the present. My heart is racing, and I see my hands shaking. That wasn't a dream, that wasn't a dream at all. I'm losing my mind and there is nothing I can do about it. I don't want to burden Jeremy with it. *Oh God, what if he decides to leave me with hearing this and seeing what's in the folder? I don't want to lose him; besides my adoptive parents, he is the absolute best thing to happen to me. And I know, I know, so cliché! Adoptive girl, with a troubled past, falls for the good guy wanting to break free of his strict parents and actually live life. Now, how many of those stories end with the couple living happily ever after...? Don't ask me the exact statistic on it, but I know it doesn't look good for me. Stop it, Poppie, you're psyching yourself out for absolutely no reason. Jeremy deserves more credit than you are giving him.*

"Poppie?" His voice is clear and solid. Bringing me out of my damning thoughts.

"Sorry, what?" The tips of my ears burning red with slight embarrassment of zoning off once again.

"You look like you're having an inner battle with yourself." He pulls over into a place called El Jefe, my stomach angrily rumbles at just the thought of food.

As I try to speak my throat is dry and scratchy, leaving me momentarily without my voice. Only once I clear my throat and slightly lick my lips does my voice return.

"I'm afraid." My voice falters and I don't say anything else.

"Tell me what's got you like this." Leaning over the emergency brake he pulls me into him the best he can. Laying my head on his shoulder I take in a few deep breaths, if I say what I feel I will be making it real. I hate this! I just want to punch something and curl up into a ball all at the same time. I want to scream and pull my hair out, but then cry and hide myself from everyone. I hate this! Ugh!

"I'm afraid you will run in the opposite direction once we see what's in that folder. And once I tell you something else, I remembered from before I was adopted. I'm just so damn terrified I'll lose you." The words spill out of my lips without my say or control.

Hands still shaking and the smell of the delicious food wafting from the restaurant teasing my stomach.

"I know what I say can only comfort you so much, because right now you are just a tightly wound ball of anxiety. So, how about I feed you first and then we go from there? Okay? Because, and now listen closely, you are absolutely worthy of my love. And more so, I will show you and reconfirm how I feel whenever you ask and even when you don't. I will do my damnedest to never let you feel that you'll lose me. Now, let's get you in there before your stomach thinks your throat has been cut." With a sarcastic smile and truth in his eyes, he squeezes my hand, and we walk into the restaurant. Being engulfed by such delicious smells and lively chatter brings an unconscious smile to my face, fully taking charge of all my thoughts.

Chapter Six
I Was What!?!

It was the next morning, we were going to stay an extra day considering we got what we came for quicker than either one of us would have guessed. I never did end up opening my file last night. Every time I attempted to read about myself, I ended up opening the folder then immediately closing it and slamming it back down on the table and huffing in disgust with myself. This was absolute bullshit! I just need to get over myself and see what it says about me. *Dammit all to hell! Get yourself together Poppie! Your file is not going to read itself!*

"Do you want me to go get you a 'pick me up drink' before you open it?" Jeremy stretches what's left of sleep lingering, only being up for about twenty minutes.

"No, I just need to mentally slap myself out of my own thoughts. You know, just grab my shoulders and shake myself until I don't know up from down." I do a ridiculous shaking movement with my arms and adding a funny noise with my vocal chords.

"That looks absolutely terrifying! I wouldn't do that if I were you." Teasing me, he laughs. His laughter releasing the built-up tension in me, I finally do it.

Opening the folder to view my file, slowly I read so I can process what is being stated.

In bold red, the first thing written on the page, reads: F.B.I. Personnel Clearance Only.

Shit that judge must have worked through a lot of red tape to get this information and yet was kind enough to not make me jump through anymore hoops to have the file. What the hell could have been so damn important that the F.B.I. would get involved? Reading on I soon get my answers. The most disturbing answers one could get. What I read before me makes my mouth go dry and my stomach knot. Feeling the urge to vomit, I close my eyes taking a deep breath. Opening my eyes once again I start reading out loud, as if making these words on the file become real.

Jane Doe, six years of age, severely malnourished; full work up from examiner shows further indicators of years of abuse. Only known relatives are Ellis and David Morningstar. However, Jane Doe cannot remember her own name. When asking the Morningstars they said they never cared enough to learn or remember her name Mr. Morningstar openly admitted. Grandparents sold her to well-known child trafficking ring run by the Mirth brothers. Mr. and Mrs. Morningstar are serving time for abuse, neglect, and child endangerment. Mirth brothers got away, but all known affiliates taken into custody.

Jane Doe called Twenty-seven and over half a dozen other kids of all ages recovered. Unknown damages have occurred, and the aftermath can be catastrophic for all involved.

"Shit, Jer, my memory I told you about yesterday, it was real. I'm not losing my mind. And that reoccurring nightmare, must have actually happened." Before he can process everything and reply I'm already reading on more. Again, reading aloud.

F.B.I. agents Mr. and Mrs. Raven headed the team that disbanded the underground ring. After months of proceedings on both the conflict of interest in their line of work and the routine steps with the adoption agency, were finally able to adopt Jane Doe aka Twenty-seven.

"Jer, do you hear this?" I start to hyperventilate. "I was FUCKING SOLD! Who the hell does that!?! I was their bloody granddaughter for fuck's sake! And my own parents didn't even want me either? I don't get it, what did I ever do to them for my own parents to not want me?"

"Your mom and dad are F.B.I.? Did you know?" calmly he asks, still dumbstruck at the information he has just read.

"I had no idea, honest. I can't believe I never knew what they did for me. But why didn't they tell me when I confided in them about what was going on? How could they not tell me? They had to have known that my problems wouldn't just go away with the bi-weekly therapy sessions. I mean, damnit, I'm so fucked up!"

"You're not fucked up. You had an absolutely horrific past and demons today because of it, but you are not fucked up. It's your bio parents and grandparents that are the fucked-up ones. I promise, there is absolutely nothing wrong with you." Gently taking the folder out of my hands and setting it down on the table, he looks me dead in the eye. "Please don't hurt my girlfriend by saying these bad things about her."

"I know I'm the one who wanted to stay today and head out tomorrow, but could we actually leave today. I kind of want to get out of here as quickly as possible. I just want to take a shower before we leave. And maybe stopping at a store before we head out. There is something I need to get before we start our trek home." Standing up, I stretch and here my spine cracks all the way up.

"Yah, I'll pack our stuff while you shower and then we can head out." Smiling, he quickly smacks my butt as I walk away.

The shower turned to the max heat feels wonderful. The pain from the hot water does a kind of deep tissue massage and releases all existing tightness of my muscles. Not wanting to get out I wait until the water is nerve ending numb with an after effect of blue lips. I don't feel it though, my mind too far down the rabbit hole, trying to process everything I just learned. Hyper focusing on every little detail, trying to commit it to memory. It's classic case of 'analyze to paralyze', but no matter how hard I try to stop myself, here I am.

"Hey, babe, aren't you freezing? This bathroom feels like a walk-in meat locker. Damn." Not hearing him come in I jump at his words.

"Shit, Jer, you scared the hell out of me! I hit my funny bone … Ow." A mix between a groan and laugh escapes my lips. Rubbing my elbow to ease the vibrations running through my arm, my thoughts try to slip back to those black/white and red taunting words within that damned file. It's taunting me isn't even the worst thing. What is even worse is I know I will go over that file until I can recite it in my sleep.

***

Before leaving town, we stopped at a department store and picked me up a blanket. There is nothing better than an Adirondack 100% polyester plush blanket. I have one at home that I forgot to pack for this trip. Considering I can't cuddle up next to Jeremy while he drives, it's the next best thing for the sense of comfort I crave. It's by no means cold out, so I roll down my window halfway. Only curling up to the blanket, not laying it over me. I close my eyes and let the wind wisp against my face.

It's only been a couple hours on the road before Jeremy pulls off the highway, needing a break to stretch and buy an energy drink. I can see he's tired and his muscles are tense. Not to mention I can see bags forming underneath his eyes. I think all this information is hitting him just as hard as it is me. This man next to me, loves me so deeply that he'd take all my pain just so I wouldn't have to carry it alone.

"Jer, let me take the wheel for a while. Yours eyes must be killing you for having to stay focused on nothing but the road for so long. And you drove all the way here, so I can drive us some on the way home."

"Babe, it's no problem. Besides, you are in no state to be driving. There was so much for you to take in, you just need to be able to process the information and not worrying about driving."

"Actually, I need the distraction. I've been going over the file over and over again, but I can't put it down. Let me drive."

"Poppie, let's not have an argument over this, okay."

"No. Not okay. You're disregarding your own health for me and quite frankly I don't like being patronized and being told how I need to process all this information."

Standing just outside of the convenience store next to his car, the wind is slightly blowing making my hair flow in a few different directions. Which is only pissing me off more in my irritated state. To calm the flurry that is my hair, I pull my hair into a side braid. Only realizing too late that I don't have a hair tie. Quickly looking on my wrists, feeling my pockets and looking on my seat in desperate need. Frustratingly coming up empty handed. Jeremy steps a little closer with his hand outstretched to me, with a small black hair tie in his hand. Sporting a devilishly handsome sly smile and even though we aren't currently happy with each other, we still share this moment.

"Perks of having the best boyfriend ever. Knowing you, I always have a couple on me. I know you hate the way your hair messily gets in your face."

"Awe, Jer! You are most definitely the best." Tying off the end of the braid, I wrap my arms around his neck and quickly peck his lips.

"Fucking hell, Poppie, answer me this. Do you actually want to drive? Yes or no, only."

"No, I really don't want to, but I don't want to be needy and desperate. And, to add to it, I feel like I'm being a bad girlfriend. Because, I drag you out here, and my dark past, as well with all my terrifying nightmares that might actually hold more truth to them than most people's do. I just… I just love you so incredibly much and worry that I'm not good enough for you. Because you deserve the best and I'm just a mess." My voice breaks as I'm rambling with silent tears running down my cheeks. I can only imagine what I look like. It's just everything I said holds 100% truth. I can feel an anxiety attack coming, and per my usual, I want food to munch on. Having a bottomless pit of a need to eat.

Grabbing one of the teriyaki Jerky sticks we bought, I start chewing away while taking in calming breaths. I mean my parents abandoned me with my grandparents, who then sold me into a child sex trafficking ring. Then to be saved and adopted by an F.B.I. married couple. Fuck. I always just thought something happened to my bio parents and that's why I was put into foster care. Not to mention I never even had any idea my mom and dad were F.B.I., I thought they were boring mundane people.

"Poppie, you've got some unbelievably crazy shit happening to you, but that doesn't define you. It helped in making you who you are today, but it's not all you are. I know that you love me as much as I love you. And listen to what I'm about to tell you, because it's something I want you to always remember. You ARE worth it. No matter what, always." As he says this, he looks me directly in the eyes, they are showing no hesitation. No sign that the words coming out of his mouth to be a lie. Only warmth and love being expressed. Jeremy is humble, kind, smart, funny, and then as a cherry on top good looking. Oh and let's not forget overprotective, which I love, and adventurous. This wonderful guy, I'll give my life just for him to know how much I love him.

"And now I know you are too good for me." I smile widely at him and start a low laugh. I see a smile form on his face.

"Now, get your cute ass in the car and let's get home. Shall we?" kissing me, he opens my door and shuts it behind me as I climb in.

***

With everything I've discovered about myself and my past, I'm weirdly finding myself content as we make our journey home. Having steady conversation amongst the long periods of pleasant silence. I have come to accept that my questions have been answered and not everything will be solved so easily.

Chapter Seven
Heart Wrenching Confrontation

It's been a week since Jer and I got home, and I've shamefully been avoiding and ignoring my parents. I don't know how to talk to them right now. With the emotions involved, disappointment being the most prominent, I would probably blow up in their faces and say something I know I would regret.

Although, that hasn't stopped them from trying to get ahold of me. Taking it as far as getting ahold of Jer and having him talk to me, being a messenger for them. I wish they would understand that I need time, time, and space.

Laying on Jeremy's couch with his arms around me. I can feel the rhythm of his heartbeat, effortlessly calming me with its calm soft beats. We're watching the horror movie, *Prom Night*, it's one of my favorites. The scene we're on is the one with the girl on the construction floor of the motel; my phone goes off, making me jump in my seat. The caller I.D. says that it's Dad. Looking at his goofy smile for his contact photo I remember the day I took this photo of him, making a smile force its way onto my face even though my mind is at war with my emotions.

Sighing I know that Mom is sitting right there next to him.

"Babe, you should talk to them. Even if it's only to yell at them, anything is better than this radio silence. I think they are worried they are going to lose you because of this."

"You're absolutely right. I don't want them to have that worry because no matter what they are my parents. Would you go with me to talk with them?" A heavy sigh escapes through my lips. *No time like the present to fix this, Poppie*.

"Of course, anything you want Poppie."

***

The drive to my parents is agonizingly slow and yet at the same time impossibly quick; neither of which have given me any time to think about how to start a conversation with my parents. As we come to a stop at the last stop sign before their house, I can already see the house and my parents out on the front porch with mugs in their hands.

I didn't talk to them ahead of time to let them know we were coming over, so they are just enjoying this beautiful Saturday with the weather only reaching 80°. They haven't seen us pull up yet, but my palms are already sweaty, and my hands are shaking. Then as a trifecta my brain has decided to shut down and lock me out.

Sitting there all I can focus on my breathing, calm deep breathing, in… and out. A gust of warm air alerts me that my door has been opened, abruptly bringing me out of the rabbit hole that is my thoughts.

No, I'm not ready yet. I don't want to see the disappointment, anger, or sadness in their eyes. What if they hate me for not just dropping the whole thing?

"Come on, Poppie, the sooner you talk to them the sooner you can move forward from it. They love you, and you love them."

"What if they can't get over the fact that I didn't just drop all this? Not to mention, I'm still hurt that they didn't just tell me all this themselves. It breaks my heart that I had to find out from strangers and not my own parents. All we are going to do is sit in complete awkward silence, with you being the one to try to lighten the mood."

"And you are stalling, which is counterproductive and as much as I love you and would take you back home in a heartbeat I can't, because your parents have seen us now for the past two minutes talking but not moving their direction."

"Shit. Shit. Shit. I guess it's time to rip off the tacky months old band aid."

Jeremy stifles a fit of laughter at my metaphor for this whole ordeal, as he helps me out of the car, and we cross the street. Walking up the stone steps of the house I grew up in, I have never been more anxious while ascending these steps. Right as I am halfway up the steps my clumsy self misses a step, causing me to fall forward. Cursing under my breath as sharp pain shoots through my shin. Moments later I feel cold air on raw skin and a warm trickle down my leg. There is a blood stain at the source of my wound and after my pants absorbed all it could in that spot, there is a line of blood going down the pant leg.

"Well I guess this is as good as any for an ice breaker. Poppie, how about you get cleaned up and then we'll talk." Mom squeezes my hand once we are in front of them at the white metal painted table. White is such an ugly color and stains the easiest.

"Yah, we'll be down in a second. Jeremy, would you help me up the stairs and to my old room?"

"How about you hop on my back and I'll give you a piggyback ride?" Jeremy squats down so I don't have to put strain on my leg. He is so silly; I love him so much.

Once we are upstairs in my old room, I grab a pair of pants that I left behind as spares for when I come over, then I head to the bathroom attached to my room.

Jeremy brings over a warm wet rag as I wait sitting on the counter no longer in my pants and hilariously showing the forest growing on my legs.

"Hey, babe, you know I could shave these monstrosities for you if you need." He laughs as he gently takes care of my wound for me. Laughing at his playful comment, I stick my tongue out at him.

***

We've been at my parents' house for over an hour and our conversation has gone from silent enough to hear a pin drop in a zoo to louder than an illegal street race with loud music, revving cars and people talking and making bets. It all reminded me of the episode of *Gilmore Girls* where Richard and Emily confront Rory and Lorelai about Rory having resentment to Emily for breaking Lorelai and Luke up, with Emily blaming Rory's attitude on Lorelai and they move from room to room until the argument has died down and the problem has been resolved.

Yah, that's exactly how this felt.

"You don't get it; I needed these answers and you guys obviously weren't going to tell me!" I feel like pulling my hair out. All we are doing is going around in circles, a vicious never-ending cycle.

"Do you not get it? The brothers that run the ring got away and you looking into it can put you in danger. They have eyes and ears everywhere; it wouldn't be totally impossible for them to have a man on the inside at the agency," Mom shouts.

"Your mother is absolutely right, you put yourself in danger." Dad always the one in the middle trying his damnedest to calm us both. Dad has always been somewhat of the peacemaker in our family. Not saying that Mom and I don't have a good relationship, because we do, but when we get into it, we both are strong willed and hard headed.

"That's exactly my point. If you guys had just told me yourselves, I wouldn't have had to put myself in that danger."

"Poppie, give your mom and I a break. This is not a normal adoptive family situation. We were flying blindly all these years. We took you to therapy for years hoping that it was the right decision, and that it would help you process through everything. We didn't know that your memories would start now and not then."

"I love you both so much and will always be grateful for the life and love you have given me, but I need to go clear my head and process everything. I'll call you guys tomorrow."

"Okay, sweetie, and how about you two come over Friday for a family dinner?"

"That would be wonderful, Piper. Andrew it was great to see you again. Would you guys want to play cards or ten thousand? It's been a while."

"You are so on, Jeremy, my boy. Piper and Poppie can watch me kick your butt."

I laugh at what my dad says to Jeremy. Giving both my parents a hug I whisper in each of their ears how much I love them and that we will see them Friday.

As Jer and I walk to his car hand in hand, something across the street catches my eye. Silently I lead, dragging Jer over there with me. Having a closer look at it, it looks to be a poster for something on an old telephone pole. Getting closer still I see it's a poster for a carnival coming to the town over from us, a month from now. The details on the poster inform me that the carnival will be in town for one week and one week alone. Reading that last sentence in my head I say it with a pause and dramatic voice just for effect.

Hmmm...

...I've never been to a carnival before.

Chapter Eight
Carnival

It's been a couple weeks since my parents and I went the rounds that night. I do feel that they'll be upfront with me from now on. That thought alone is an immense weight lifted off my chest.

It's about nine a.m. on a Friday morning and I'm headed to my job at my uncle's company. Parking has always been a bitch… There is none! At least none for entry level associates… i.e. me. After finding a spot on the street that allows all day parking, my eyes are drawn to another poster for that carnival that is coming to the town over. I swear, I've seen close to a dozen since laying eyes on the first one, giving me these unignorable nagging thoughts on if I should go or not. There are just enough unknowable variables in this situation for me to be able to make a proper decision. As much as I am wanting to go, what if it unlocks more nightmares instead of helping this one come to a close?

"Good morning, Poppie. Uncle Bill would like to see you in his office once you get a moment, but he does urge as soon as possible," Lorall greets me.

"Morning, Lorall. I bought you your regular from that little coffee shop down the street that you love. How is your wedding planning going?" Taking a moment to catch up with Lorall, I can see the blush on her cheeks and the love in her eyes.

"Harrison is so invested in the details, as much as I am if not even more. It's so funny to see him talking about eggshell, burnt sienna and robin's egg coloring. Even for me, I see green when he sees emerald," Lorall giggles. "Damn do I love that man. I myself don't want to wear white on our wedding day, it's not my color nor do I want to stain it, but I know he'd love to see me in white. He hasn't outwardly said it, knowing that I have an aversion to the color. I might just have to dress in white to surprise him. I am only getting married once so why not, right?"

"You guys are so cute together. Anyway, I should go talk with Uncle Bill, but keep me up to date please!" quickly walking towards the elevator I holler back at her. Hearing Lorall laugh makes me smile from ear to ear. Lorall and I are extremely close, she and I are cousins and Uncle Bill is both our uncle. Our family company is Uncle Bill at the top and anyone who is family that works here got here of their own hard work. Uncle Bill is a completely devoted family man. So my hook up is just an assistant while in college, but he knows I might not be here afterwards. Though, you damn well know I work my ass off to earn my job, showing him I will be my absolute best.

Ding

Hearing the alert that the elevator reached my desired floor level, I'm brought out of my thoughts of Lorall's wedding and everywhere else my mind wandered off to. I knock on my uncle's cedar office door and wait until I hear a clear firm voice telling me to enter.

"Poppie!"

"Uncle Bill!" I run over and am pulled into a bear hug. I forgot to mention today is the first day of working for the summer. So it's been a month or two since we've had a big family dinner with him.

"Sorry to corner you, but your mom and dad told me about everything that has happened recently. I'm sorry they didn't tell you themselves about what went down. I was quite shocked myself hearing everything you went through before they adopted you. I didn't even know they were government agents." Uncle Bill adjusts the glasses on the bridge of his nose, sighing as if to relieve an oncoming headache.

"Mom, Dad, and I definitely went the rounds that night, I felt so betrayed by them and alone. Jeremy was really a rock for me, but he also helped me see things from their side. I have so many more questions about it all and don…"

My words get cut off by the carnival poster peeking out underneath some paperwork on his desk. It's everywhere! Bloody Hell!

"What's this?" Pulling it out from under the papers I look it over once again for the tenth time at least.

"Oh yeah, June and I thought it would be a great family night out with the twins; Liam and Margot have been bugging us about going, so we thought why not." He laughs.

"I was thinking of going with Jer, for a purely educational reasoning though. It might be able to dredge up some repressed memories and hopefully making some fun new memories to out shadow the old ones. So we might run into you guys there if we end up going on the same night."

"Well best luck to you on that, and I truly mean it. Now that I've seen you and been able to catch up let's continue on with work shall we."

"On the double, Uncle Bill!" I mock salute him, trying to keep a straight face. However, failing miserably as a soft smile graces my face shortly after seeing the cheeky grin on his.

Handing him back the poster I walk to my desk outside his office and start getting to work and making the separate preorder calls for mine and Uncle Bill's lunches.

***

The first day of the carnival is tomorrow Saturday and goes through until midnight on the following Friday. Maybe I can talk Jer into a date night at this carnival. Excitement flows through me at the thought.

It's already six, I'm waiting as patiently as I can for Jer to get off work and come over. I'm getting very antsy though and with my roommate being particularly annoying tonight, it's grinding on my nerves and patience. She's currently channel surfing through Netflix, getting ten to fifteen minutes into a show or movie then deciding to change it. This normally doesn't affect me whatsoever, so I'm trying my hardest to keep my nerves in check. Checking my phone again for the time, I sigh in impatience.

Thump, thump, thump, thump, thump... thump, thump. The rhythmic knocking of 'shave and a haircut' can only be one person. Jeremy! Finally!

"Jer! You know I love that movie, especially that scene. Come in, come in. I have something to talk to you about. There is a carnival happening a town over; it's open from tomorrow to next Friday, one p.m. to twelve a.m. I really crave new memories to replace my current ones. Will you go with me? It can be a date for us."

"Hmm… One condition. If we do this, we leave the moment I feel uncomfortable with how it is affecting you. Deal?"

"Deal, but within reason. Give me at least ten minutes, even if I seem a little off. Okay? Just a few minutes to get comfortable."

"Deal."

We shake hands with comically straight faces, ones that neither of us can keep. Sadly yet not sadly at all I break before Jer does.

“Now, I know tomorrow is the grand opening and there will be an insane amount of people and kids hopped up on sugar, buuutttt, can we go anyway! I don’t want to wait, I’ve been seeing these posters for it all over town since the night you, Mom, Dad, and I sat down to hash out our feelings and now I’m simply bursting at the seams to go.”

“Well with the sugar crazed kids and the masses of people are real seller points for going on opening day. Can’t go on a day with a tornado? Wouldn’t that be easier?” Jer plays with me, laughter in his voice.

“Babe, of course we can go tomorrow. We just need to stick together so we don’t wind up separated. Also, we need to fully charge both our cells just in case we do end up getting separated, we don’t want dead phones. Plus, we need a backup plan on where to meet in case luck really isn’t on our side tomorrow. I’m really worried about this and this will help ease my mind, so just bear with me while I’m in my overprotective boyfriend mode.”

I absolutely adore this side of him. Jeremy is a very even keeled protective gruff of a man. He doesn’t squash me down as an independent individual. More so what he does is make sure I don’t do reckless shenanigans alone; keeping an eye to call when is when.

Spending the evening together, we order take out and play card games until we end up calling it a night.

Now, the carnival count down is on, so on!

***

'She take my money, well I'm in need.' *Gold Digger* by Kanye West starts playing through the speaker on my phone as my alarm. Bringing a refreshed smile to my face, excitement courses through me producing natural adrenaline, turning me into a kid hopped up on sugar. Turning over in Jeremy's arms to face him, I breathe him in. It's all him, he doesn't wear any cologne, just deodorant. Even asleep, he has a calming effect. Yes, Jeremy is the one for me. I've known that without a doubt since the moment we decided to be with each other.

"You know, we could stay like this all day. In bed, quality time watching TV or talking, anything you want."

"So tempting, on such a real level tempting. How about no more than three hours at the carnival, then the rest of the day we do whatever you want. No matter what that is. Promise." Laying on his chest I offer him my right pinky finger. With me laying on his right side, he offers me his left pinky. Accepting it we do an awkward pinky promise, laughing at how we have to do it.

***

After a forty-minute drive and a $12 parking fee we've finally made it. Only to have to wait in what I could only describe as a mile-long line; in one-hundred-degree weather.

"Water! Water! Get your water here! A dollar-fifty a bottle!" A couple of carnie vendors walk down the customer line. Of course a great way to make easy profit, telling us no outside food or drink allowed, then using it against us desperate dehydrated folk. A dollar-fifty isn't much but I'm good, I can wait until we get through the gates. Then again this might possibly be half priced. I've heard water can get $3 or more at these events.

"-oppy. Here, I got us each a bottle." Looks like I got lost in my thoughts long enough to miss the whole interaction Jer had with the vendor. Damn, that's some deep concentration. He must have seen the internal debate going on in my head by my facial expression. Giving me a simple smile while uncapping his bottle and taking a drink.

Looking back in front of me to see how far the line had moved up it seems like we were next; thankfully, they had two separate windows to purchase tickets from. The lady didn't look to amused at the crowd. People must have already broken down her tolerance for the moment anyway.

"Good afternoon, could we get two all access passes, please."

"Those would be our bracelets and those are $25 apiece."

Pulling out three twenties handing it over, I politely ask her for two fives back. She gives me a tired sigh handing me the change and our bracelets. I smile brightly at her thanking her and handing her one of the $5 bills as a tip. It's really not much of a tip, and that's assuming that workers here even get tips but as of right now her and the other ticket person have dealt with the brunt of the masses. I didn't need to say anything to go with it, because actions speak louder than words and saying anything would defeat my kindness.

"Babe, I'm going to buy the food we eat here today since you took care of the bracelets."

"Sounds like a plan to me. I wonder if there is a photo booth, we could get our pictures taken? Where should we start first?"

"How about some cotton candy, then walk around to see what there is? After we know all the attractions we can choose." Nodding in approval, we go hunt down the cotton candy stand.

It's almost suffocating here even though this is an outside event. The number of people here are causing my heart rate to increase and my mind to become fuzzy. Latching on to Jeremy's arm I close my eyes letting him lead me. I block everything around me out of my mind so I can calm down. Instead, I focus on the grass beneath my feet and the smells filtering through the air. Keeping in mind to not take note of all the overwhelming sounds. *Breathe*.

“What can I get for the two of you?” Hearing an unfamiliar male voice brings me back to what is going on in front of me. I exhale all negative emotions from my system.

“We will take a mixed bag please and thank you. Do you also by any chance have any napkins.” As Jer tells the man what we’d like I wonder what color I’m going to make my tongue. Pink won’t really change its color, blue it is!

“I know we just got here but after the moment you had a few minutes ago, we can leave if you want.”

“Nope, what I want is to see how blue I can turn my tongue. So you’re gonna have to fight me for any of that color.” I snag the bag of cotton candy and run off into the hall of mirrors that was across the way from us, laughing as I get him to chase me.

“Catch me if you can!” Turning a few corners before I stop in front of a mirror that makes you look dwarfish and chunky. Only stopping to enjoy the contraband in my hands.

“Marco!” I stop eating like a deer caught in the headlights.

“Come find me, Polo! I might just eat all this by myself!” seeing two different directions, besides the way I came, to choose from. Closing my eyes, I spin around enough to lose my bearings and then chose a random direction to take. I’m only on my way for about a minute before Jeremy catches up to me. Backing me up against a mirror and boxing me in between his arms,

I see the fire in his eyes as he smiles at me goofily. Neither one of us say anything just breathing in each other's air. My heart races at the position and close proximity between us.

"We have to behave ourselves or we might just have to ditch this place and find somewhere private. I am trying to behave, but you are making it damn hard on me." Still smiling with his eyes closed he breathes out.

"I am behaving, I'm wearing pants and a tank top. Have you seen some of the outfits the girls here are wearing. You're lucky I'm modest enough not to drive you crazy with my clothing. I can't promise to behave any further than that," my hands resting on his hips, teasingly slipping my hands underneath the bottom of his shirt, but not moving them from that spot. I don't want to torture the poor guy too much, only just a little.

After a few minutes of cooling down in the hall of mirrors; with only a few carnival goers passing through, we make it through the maze. Once outside we play a couple simple vendor games, we get drawn in to one of the main event tents.

"Come one, come all! Be amongst the first to see our main attraction! The show begins in fifteen minutes, so don't miss out!" The voice sends eerie chills down my spine, sending my heart rate up and causing my palms to sweat and a slight tremor to start in my hands. I don't like the vibe this man is sending off in overwhelming waves. I can't tell Jer though, we have been having a blast. I just need to keep it to myself and just be more aware of my surroundings. *Breathe, Poppie.*

As the man repeats his spiel, I follow Jeremy into the tent. The first thing that hits me is that it's at least fifteen degrees cooler, next is the crowd that has been drawn in. It's not too full in here, letting us find perfect seating.

By the time we are settled and bought popcorn off a vendor walking around the tent, the announcer brings our attention to him in the middle of the tent. I see a man with heterochromia and a shaved head. An overall strange sight, but fear strikes through me as I recognize the man from my memories as well as my government file. Though from when I knew him before, he had a full head of hair.

I'm frozen to my spot as he starts to speak loud and with practiced excitement, knowing just what to say to amp up the crowd. Observing how he feeds off all the positive cheers.

Me though, hands shaking, throat closing and silent tears flowing down my cheeks unchecked. My past has come back to haunt me. The man being one of the Mirth brothers that had escaped the F.B.I raid all those years ago.

"And for all those who have our platinum passes after the show we have set up an exclusive tour and meet and greet. So stay seated. Now with no further ado our first act!" the man announces.

"Jeremy get me out of here now!" I grit through clenched teeth, but it barely comes out as a distressed whisper. Until now Jeremy was entranced by all the flare. Looking over my emotional state he becomes very aware of my mental state.

"Poppie, can you walk out of h—?

"I-I-I can't m-move, please…" Not making me say anything more and not saying anything himself he carries me out of the tent, through the carnival grounds and out to the car bridal style. With my head laying on his chest, eyes closed and listening to his heartbeat. I block everything else out. I cannot fucking believe what I saw back there. Could they really have hidden as carnies for this long? Was this how they built an alibi for all those years while buying and selling children? Even closing my eyes I can see his demonic gaze etched on the inside of my eyelids.

Chapter Nine
Platinum Passes

The entire drive home was absolutely quiet, and so was the rest of the evening. I couldn't bring myself to share what I saw. I felt so dead inside. So completely overwhelmed and there was no end to my tears staining my cheeks. Jeremy had tried to talk to me a couple times to no avail. As my stomach growled, I realized I hadn't eaten anything since the cotton candy and a few bites of popcorn. Though as my stomach rumbled, my eyes traveled to the time on my phone, making me realize it was already after nine. I couldn't bring myself to get up to eat, in fact I had no appetite even with how hungry I was.

With my eyes wandering around my room I take in the tray of now cold food. It seems Jeremy has left; my roommate was staying the night at her girlfriend's house. It was their anniversary today, making the rest of the house quiet. I didn't hear Jeremy at all leading to my previous conclusion. Dull feeling of pain coursing through me knowing he is not here, even with the fact that I've shut him out for over five hours.

"I don't know what to do. She told me to get her out of there, and since then it has been radio silence with her. I don't know what she saw or heard, and she's refused to eat. I need your help. Please…"

I hear Jeremy's voice and just know that he is talking to my parents. I hear all three sets of feet, telling me that they are all here. *'Fix the broken, I dare you.'* Morbidly I think to myself. I close my eyes again to pretend I'm still asleep. Hoping to get them to leave me the hell alone. I don't like this anger that has settled in me, but I do nothing to stop myself from feeling it either.

"Baby, wake up, baby. Your mom and dad are here, we are all worried about you, love." Blankly I open my eyes to look at them, but not seeing them, only seeing through them. I hear a snapping sound rigidly grinding against my ear drums. It causes me to curl in a ball and put my head in the crook of my arms in an attempt to be anywhere but here. The warmth of the blankets covering me that normally give me the comfort I seek is even lost on me now.

"Poppie, you have to give us something, sweetheart. Please!" Jeremy painfully pleads with me, pulling me into his arms as he sits back against the headboard. Panicking at any form of touch, stuck back in my past as a six-year-old being at the abandoned carnival grounds. I'm no longer in my room with Jeremy and my parents.

'Tweny-seven I told you to finish your food! You think you're better than all the other kids here, and that you don't have to eat what we give you.' The older Mirth

brother back hands me across the face, causing my head to snap to side. His two different color eyes scare me the most about him. So shallow and eerie.

With tears silently sliding down my face I pick up my fork and start eating what is on my plate. It's not the worst he's done to me, but I don't want to anger him further than I already have. Looking up I lock eyes with Eighteen; I can see she wants to comfort me, but she can't, or she will be punished as well. The food in my mouth is growing in size, making it impossible to swallow. The more I chew the drier my mouth becomes. I have both the Mirth brothers watching me intently. In fact all eyes are on me, those of the kids are sneaking glances while the Mirth brothers are violent daring stares. Everyone one of us knowing what'll happen if I don't cooperate. With all the dryness in my throat and mouth it causes me to gag the first two attempts at swallowing. By the third try I manage to choke it down. With unsteady hands I scoop up another bite. Looking at the prospect ahead of me a whimper dies in my dry throat before it can reach the ears of those around me. I feel taunted as all the kids around me still have their cups of water. My cup was taken from me at the first sight of struggle over having to eat what they considered acceptable food that was put in front of me. As the older Mirth brother goes to gab at me, I scream for him to stop. I'm eating like they want me to; I can't help the gagging that is happening.

'No, don't touch me! Stop, I promise I'll eat! Stop!'

"Stop! Please, stop!" I come back to the present, feeling compression around my arms and chest. It's a calming method that brings me back and works perfectly every time. Though, this is the first time it has been used to bring me back from a previously suppressed memory.

"Poppie, can you tell your dad and I what happened today at the carnival? Did being there bring up some bad memories? Talk to us, please," Mom, pleads with me.

"M-m-momma, h-he was there. The older Mirth brother. I-I saw him in the tent. In the file it said you guys never caught him or his brother." I hand her the flyer for the carnival with shaky hands.

"Poppie, they can't hurt you any more."

"That doesn't mean they still can't hurt kids! You guys just gave up! Let them get away! Bad people don't just change because their operation gets busted. How could you not catch them?" I break down into a sobbing mess. It's not safe for kids and a carnival is prime hunting grounds for their scheme.

"Come one! Come all! In town for one week. Attention all with pre-purchased platinum passes; exclusive tour and meet and greet after first showtime on the first day of carnival." My dad reads out most of what was on the flyer. I didn't even realize that he had the flyer. His voice had become tight with emotion when talking about the passes; by the looks of his white knuckles holding the paper something written on the paper triggered him. Looking between him and Mom they're both silently speaking with their eyes. Whatever it is can't be anything good.

"Dad, Mom," both snap their head to me, but the silence still lingers between them.

"Ahem, Poppie, while you were in that tent did you hear anything about these platinum passes?"

"No, Dad, I didn't…Wait! I did, but all it was, was the word platinum passes, by the point he was mentioning it I was already mentally gone. What does that have to do with anything anyways?" Puzzled I look at Jer to see if he heard what it was about.

"All it was, was a private tour and meet and greet. Nothing special there." Jeremy speaks up answering the question.

"It is though; back even before we got you and ended that operation, it was a common cover up for the child trafficking. See what it is, is their way of showing kids while there is something huge going on to distract everyone else. Then those with platinum passes would go to where the kids were being held and be sold off. Then the buyer would walk through the crowd with what looked like an asleep child. Though the child wasn't asleep in the normal sense of the word. They would be chloroformed so they wouldn't bring attention to themselves. The only thing we could never quite figure out was if all the carnies were in on it or not. We don't believe they were though." Hearing the well thought out scheme that the Mirth brothers have makes me nauseous and I think Dad can tell, because by the end of his explanation he got quieter and quieter, almost like he didn't want to be telling me this.

My emotions are so haywire, I just want to slip into a coma and sleep through this nightmare

***

Mom and Dad both left shortly after that with the persuasion of Jer. I was drained and couldn't function as a human being for the rest of the night. Jeremy stayed even with my protest; I couldn't even function to be a good girlfriend. I think he knew that and decided to stay mainly because of that, having obvious anxiety of leaving me alone with my state of mind.

The next day after Jer left I locked myself in my room only coming out for food or the restroom. I didn't even bother to shower or brush my teeth. All I could do was replay everything from my memory as a child and from going to the carnival. At one point during the week Camille decided to go stay with her girlfriend; it was that bad.

It's Saturday morning, exactly a week after going to the carnival. I can't do this anymore! I want to forget; I want to be normal.

I'm brought out of my thoughts as I hear the whistle of the tea kettle. After pouring the hot water in my cup I set the kettle down on a cool burner. The red color, from the still hot burner catches my eye and all thought leaves my head. My hand with a mind of its own slowly makes its way downwards to the coiled surface of the coiled electric stove. Feeling the harsh thumping of my heart in my chest and my short breaths, but none of that matters as my hand still steadily with not an ounce of shaking, makes its way closer. Only when my hand is about an inch away from the surface do I snap out of the daze.

Hurting myself is not the answer. It'll only get me sent to therapy or worse the psych ward. I don't need or want that. I do need information though…

It's only five hours later that I'm looking up from my laptop. I've looked up child trafficking spikes in coordination with carnival stops. As well as how long this specific carnival has been in business. The only thing I can't get concrete proof on is it being linked to the Mirth brothers.

Currently, I'm looking at group photos of the carnival when one of the photos catches my eye. It's him! The guy making the first announcement getting us into the tent that day.

Life definitely wasn't kind to him. I don't get how he wasn't saved that day that I was too. Did the F.B.I. really not save all the kids. Who else didn't make it out safe? Oh God! I hope Eighteen was saved.

Glancing back at the photo there is a name for everyone in the photo. Underneath Twenty was the name Austin. I wonder if that is his real name or the one, they gave him.

Impulsively and irrationally, I group text my parents: 'you didn't save all of them?!'

As I wait for a reply from either of them, I pace the floor in my room impatiently. After only waiting mere minutes, I decide to shower the stink off me. Damn I smell absolutely dreadful. Walking to my bedroom door a low soundless vibration stops me. Quickly I walk back to my phone, the screen waking up as I hold it in my hands. My eyebrows scrunch as I look at the blank lock screen.

"But I could have sworn that… ugh." Am I imagining things in my paranoid state? I just want all this to be over so badly. Checking that the volume is indeed on and at high volume, I throw my phone back down onto my bed. Not worried that it might break because it's my bed not an elementary school playground blacktop. Halfway across my bedroom I huff, turn around, and grab my phone taking it into the bathroom with me.

Once I see the steam clouding the bathroom, I know it's just what I need and hop in. Maybe I can get just a few minutes of peace from my overwhelming thoughts.

Chapter Ten
Therapy?

I've ordered my Chinese comfort food for dinner and am now waiting for it to arrive. I've heard my phone go off another three times while I was in the shower, but each time when I went to look, nothing. I'm seriously losing my mind here, seriously what the hell. Now as I sit here listening to it ringing, I don't believe it's really happening. My mind is just playing tricks on me and I don't care for it one bit.

I let myself miss the call another two times before I actually pick it up, answering the fourth call.

"Finally, why didn't you answer when we called any of the other times? Your father and I were getting worried."

"Sorry, my mind has been playing tricks on me since I texted you. So I wasn't sure it was really happening. Anyway, I'm assuming you read my text."

"Honey, you have to understand, your father and I tried everything we could. We were aware that the Mirth brothers got away, but we had no idea they managed to take some kids with them. You telling us is the first we have heard of it. Poppie, how did you find out? Talk to us, please."

“I did my own research; you should know that by now I will do my own digging if I don’t get the answers I want. So today I started looking into the Carnival and its history. I saw a photo of a guy I saw outside of the tent that day and underneath was a name. This time though I actually got a good look and I recognized him through his face. I know it’s without a doubt him. I wonder if I find where they are headed to next maybe I could try and talk to him. Find out if he knows what happened to any other kids that were taken with the Mirth brothers when the raid happened. Maybe see if he knows if Eighteen was saved or taken. I can’t get her off my mind. You guys should have saved her and left me behind, she needed to be saved from them. Eighteen didn’t deserve being there and she was a momma bear to us younger kids.”

“Poppie, calm down, sweetheart. Yes, she deserved to have been rescued, but that in no way means that you didn’t or that she should have and that you should have been left behind. Poppie, with all that you are going through, I think you should start going back to therapy. Your dad and I know you can’t tell us everything and feel your emotions to the fullest but talking to someone in total confidence would help you a lot.”

“What? Therapy? I’m just stressed, I don’t need to see a therapist. All I need is no judgement and support.”

“Poppie, you can’t lie to us we’ve know you since you were little. It’s not just stress, you’re hearing phantom noises from your phone, recognizing multiple faces from the carnival, and only relying on yourself. You're not even fully confiding in Jeremy at the moment. Now, I'm not trying to be mean or insensitive but for your health I think you should see a therapist. Please, honey, at least try three sessions. If at that point you find them pointless and unhelpful, then stop going."

"Fine, I'm not happy about this but I'll give it an honest try. It might take me a few days to find one I believe will fit with what I need, so I will let you know when I've found someone and set up an appointment. No bugging me about it while looking one up. Deal?"

"Deal. Now, I'm sorry to have to cut this conversation short but Dad and I have to start looking back into the case and see where it can take us with this new information you've given us. We love you, Poppie."

"Love you too, Mom and tell Dad I love him. Oh, and let me know what you are able to dig up. If I can reconnect with Eighteen even for just one time to thank her, well that would be something I'd love to have the chance at doing."

"Okay, Poppie, we'll let you know. Bye."

"Bye."

***

I'm standing in front of Jeremy's house, unsure why but anxious with clammy hands. Taking a deep breath I knock on his door three quick repetitions. Not feeling the mood being right for a 'shave and a haircut' knock that is our special knock for each other.

"Poppie? What are you doing here? I thought your ghosting me was telling me you were ending things with me."

"Oh, Jer! I'm so incredibly sorry. I've been so lost in all this; so much so that I was drowning in emotions, that when I got your messages or missed phone calls and voice messages... Well I didn't know how to function in any way more than just existing. I've only just been knocked out of my thoughts today. I'm sorry I ghosted you, you deserve so much more than me and what I can offer right now. Um... I'll leave if that's what you want. I know you need to care for your heart just as much as anyone else's and I so respect that. I won't stop loving you though if you do. I could never stop loving you, Jer." I can't look him in the eye at the end, I can't handle the rejection I just freed him to do to me. I love him enough to let him know to care for his heart even if it breaks mine.

As I try to hold back my tears, one still manages to escape running down my cheek and over my mouth, leaving a salty taste in its wake. After taking a deep breath I look up into his eyes. They are red and bloodshot; tears are rolling down his face at a more extensive rate than my own. When he speaks again his voice is hoarse and strained as if there was something lodged in his throat. It breaks my heart just hearing it and I'm the one who's done this to him.

"Fuck, Poppie… I've been hurt for the last few days of radio silence, thinking that I no longer had a place in your life. I don't want to feel that again. I don't want to end our relationship, not one bit but I need communication. That's the only way for our relationship to survive. Okay? Don't make me feel like I'm no longer important to you, because then I will have no other choice than to protect my heart and say goodbye for good."

"Oh God no! No, I won't! I promise! I've been self-absorbed with this whole thing and I'm sorry. I'll make sure I won't do it again; I've even agreed with my parents on going to therapy to help me. I want you in my life for the rest of my life and I want to be in your life for the rest of yours. And I know what I'm about to say is a bold request but… I want to move in with you. That's all I could think about on the drive over here. All I could think about was wanting to be in your arms; to wake up in your arms every morning and to fall asleep in your arms every night. And not one bit of my thoughts scare me; that's how I know without a doubt in my heart that I am head over heels shoot for the stars in love with you. I am so sure of my love for you that I'm ready to marry you whenever you are ready to marry me. And I hope I'm not scaring you away with the talk of marriage, but I had to lay it all out." I all but shout out my proclamation at him, with my hands on his face wiping away tears from his face as he holds me tight to him.

As I think more and more of marrying Jeremy, I feel warmth spread throughout my entire body. He is my home; now don't get me wrong I love my parents and I will always have a home with them, but this is a different kind of home, rightfully its own.

"Are you asking me to marry you, Poppie Blithe Raven? If you are indeed asking me to marry you, then I have something to give you." His eyes are begging what I've told him to be true; he wants me to be his forever as much as I want him to be mine. I brightly smile up at him nodding my head yes, silently confirming his question.

In a flash he dashes off to his room, leaving me a smiling mess in his entry way. Closing the front door behind me I go to the kitchen and pour two cups of water and sit on a bar stool at the counter. I've managed to empty my cup and go back for a second by the time Jeremy walks into the room. I hadn't realized how dehydrated I was earlier; I had even started to get cotton mouth.

"I got this for you before all this started and was planning on proposing once summer began, but with all this going on… Well it no longer felt like the right time, but I've held onto it for when that time was to come. Now, though, seems you beat me to the punch. However, because I don't feel the emasculation of you proposing to me, because I fucking love the fact that you proposed the question to me, I'd like you to wear this as your engagement ring." In his hand is a simple sterling silver band with a leaf design going around it. It is by far the most beautiful delicate ring I've seen in a long time, and without a doubt so me. I let Jeremy gently slip the ring onto my finger. The size is exactly right and surprisingly deceptively heavy in weight.

Once we settle on his couch in PJs and fuzzy socks we turn on *Criminal Minds*. I suggested we binge watch it starting from season one episode one and Jeremy had no objections. Absolutely and undeniably captured in our own little bubble of contentment.

Some would argue being purely content in your life is better than being happy. Happiness is fleeting, but pure contentment only a few truly achieve. I myself am a big believer of that.

I find myself distracted as the show plays; playing with his fingers mindlessly, thoughts of our bright future together fill my head.

"Jeremy Keanu Ross… Poppie Blithe Raven-Ross, hmm. No, that doesn't sound right. Poppie Blithe Ross… Perfect." Softly mumbling to myself I can't keep the smile from reaching my chapped lips. I hear a soft hum in agreement of happiness from Jeremy. My cheeks burn with the blush gracing my face; of course he heard me.

"So when would be a good time for me to move in with you?"

"Oh, so you think I'm going to say yes?"

"Of course! You wouldn't say yes to marrying me if you weren't ready to live together. In all rights living together comes before marriage. If I'm wrong, please do correct me." Giggling at his feisty mood, I entwine our hands together.

In a moment of distraction from the show, I turn my face away from Jeremy. Big mistake on my part; fingers run up and down along my sides tickling me. No mercy is given, with laughter coming from both of us and cramped up sides on my part. I don't actually hate being tickled.

***

After what ended up failing at being a two-sided tickle fest, I had such a burst of energy that I made homemade brownies topped with my special homemade cream cheese frosting. Though luck was not on my side. I had made the frosting while the brownies cooled, then I spread it across the top of the brownies. Now my downfall came when I was going to put the brownies in the fridge to let the frosting solidify before I cut into and had a piece. I had been carrying it one handed, as I got the fridge door open is when destruction hit and the whole pan fell out of my hand landing face first onto the floor.

Giving up with a frustrated huff, Jeremy pulled off the 'impossible' and salvaged the entire pan. What Jeremy had done first was used a metal pie server, cutting the brownies into manageable pieces, then gently but firmly slid it under each piece with swift determination. When all was said and done there had been two spots that the cream actually stuck with the rest coming up completely leaving nothing behind. He told me I was lucky because he had just cleaned the floor earlier that day.

Now with the brownies saved him and I were sitting back on his couch eating the delicious rich dessert.

"This dessert is the literal definition of death by sugar. Holy hell, I can't even finish off this square I cut for myself."

I am just waiting for the sugar coma to happen; wouldn't that be a sight. Too caught up in the savory food all Jer could do was give a soft moan and nod his head. This will definitely be a favored dessert making the exclusive holiday dinner list.

Chapter Eleven
Cake Tasting

It's been a couple months since I moved in with Jeremy and my parents have been digging deeper into the case. Sadly there hasn't been much progress. My parents call once a week for regular conversation and for newfound information we might have for each other. However they've hit a substantial amount of red tape and their director is breathing down their necks about proceeding with this case properly and without biased reasoning. Director Petenski from what my parents say really hopes that we find what we need, but we have to go by the book on it. Saying that even more so because they already shouldn't be involving me, but he understands why I am involved and as long as I stay on the civilian side of the search then won't stop the entire investigation. I can work with that, though it feels like these brothers and their organization are just a living print on the earth. Evidence they were there, but no trace of where they are now. It's like they know we are searching for them, but I don't understand how they would know. I was a random person in the audience who had a random panic attack. Nothing to raise suspicion. Especially, because I never went back nor did

I cause a ruckus and bring agency attention to them while they were there. My only thought is if maybe someone recognized me like I recognized Twenty. I won't call him Austin, because I have a strong feeling that is the name the Mirth brothers gave him and if I am to meet him again, I will get his real name and treat him with the respect of calling him by whatever that is.

"Poppie, try this one. It is strawberry coconut; it doesn't sound like it would taste the best but so far I think it's my favorite." Jeremy brings me back to the present. Today we are tasting wedding cakes to find the perfect one. We are about halfway through planning our wedding at this point; Jer told me that he would be willing to wait until this whole cluster fuck is settled, but absolutely fucking not. No way am I okay with that. I don't want to wait to marry him, my life will continue to move on without me if I let myself get stuck in my haunting past and us being married will not hinder anything; it will actually strengthen us and give us both the peace that nothing in life could tear us apart. So when he had given me the option, I got a little irrational and slapped him across the face and told him he was a damn fool if he thought I'd make him wait. The truth of the matter is we don't know when or even if this will ever settle.

Then when I had processed the two minutes prior, and it registered in my brain that I got physical and yelled; well I bawled my eyes out and deeply apologized for my behavior. I don't want to be the kind of person who gets physical and yells at the person they love. I didn't deserve the forgiveness Jeremy easily gave me nor do I still deserve it, but he won't hear another word of my apologies and in a comical way one day told me that if I didn't stop apologizing to him, he would get the duct tape out and put it over my mouth to shut me up. Joke's on me though because I didn't believe he would really do it and guess what. He totally did, which caused us both to erupt in laughter and after that it was like the whole ordeal was forgotten and I felt at ease with myself and him again.

"Okay, Jer, I'll give it a try. You have to try the lemon cake though, cause it might rival your strawberry coconut one." I laugh at the morphed look that is graced upon his face as I shove an unlady like size of a bite into my mouth then proceed to open my mouth and show him 'sea food' like the child I am.

"Jer! This tastes incredible, I love my lemon-flavored pastries, but this takes first place."

"I don't know about the lemon flavored one, I couldn't really taste it over the sight I was graced with when you had to show me your mouth full."

I laugh even harder at his playfully indignant attitude and kiss him on the cheek offering him another fork full of lemon cake to try uninterrupted this time. I watch his face closely to see his reaction, because I know he'll pretend to like it if it'll make me happy. Though this is about a day that is about both of us and it's how it should be. Besides, I really do like the one he likes. Noticing the slight twinge on his face is enough to tell me he doesn't care for it, though I see the wheels turning in his brain and speak up before he gets a chance to try and convince me that he is okay with the lemon cake.

"Jer, don't even try to tell me you like it, mister. This is about our big day, emphasis on the our part. I really do love the strawberry coconut one and so do you. So the only obvious choice is that one. I don't want to be a bridezilla. It'll make me so damn happy knowing you get happiness and a good time out of this process as much as I do. Okay? So no more just going along with the bride-to-be's thoughts. Deal?"

"Okay, soon-to-be Mrs. Ross." Jer emphasizes on the Mrs. part causing a cheek aching smile to stretch across my face. Every human being deserves to feel the way I do with Jer. It should be against the laws of nature to not have this.

"All right, love birds, now that we have the cake chosen you need to choose the meal as well and then we can call it quits for the day. So I'll give you two a few minutes to talk it over and if you need any ideas to help you think of something. Here is a list of popular foods that I've seen throughout my time as a wedding planner." Abby our wedding planner hands us a laminated piece of paper for us to look over and give us ideas.

***

After our cake tasting meeting with Abby, I had a therapy meeting I had to go to. I honestly do find comfort is releasing all my feelings onto a licensed professional.

"Now, Poppie, we've had a few struggles in the past month and a half or so of meetings, but I have seen great progress. Can you tell me how you feel about your captors still being at large after all this renewed time trying to hunt them down?" Dr. Kristina Deigh smoothly asks me, this isn't the first time she has asked me this question and I know it won't be the last.

"Honestly, Dr. Deigh, it is absolutely soul crushing that they are out there and still doing it to innocent children. I haven't given up yet, and I won't until they are behind bars. Every kid that felt pain or even death at their hands will have justice and I won't give up on those innocent children either. They deserve better than that. But with being totally honest with myself, I know this choice isn't completely selfless; this is my demon to conquer, and I have to see it through to the very end to get the peace I desire."

"Very good for you in knowing that on a small level this is a self-serving act, even though it is only part of the reason. I do however believe you will be exactly who you are meant to be for those children who are still being affected by those who took you."

"Thank you, I know I could say all this to my family and fiancé, but I am aware that it wouldn't be the same because they are my family; it's just not the same no matter how you look at it. I needed the professional help, and you provide that."

"That is absolutely true, I gain nothing by saying what you want to hear. I as well come from a stranger's standpoint so I may view something in a different light. Now, it looks like we only have five more minutes together today, so how about you tell me about your wedding planning?"

I speak with her on the progress made and what is still left to do, with my arms gesturing wildly while I talk and a smile on the both of our faces, it almost feels as if we are friends not doctor and patient. I do believe that is a good thing to be feeling.

Leaving her office I walk to the receptionist and schedule an appointment for two and a half weeks out per Dr. Deigh's suggestion. Dr. Deigh believes I am making great progress and that we don't necessarily need to meet every week so unless I decide to come weekly it can be scheduled further out from each visit.

I also found out that Dr. Deigh does premarital counseling, and I think I'll bring up the idea to Jeremy. I don't know honestly if we need it with everything we've been through together, but I do know it can be particularly important to do before getting married. So it doesn't hurt to see what Jeremy thinks.

Chapter Twelve
Live Theatre and a Wedding

It's Halloween today. Today is the day that Lorall and Harrison tie the knot, fully committing themselves to one another. They went with a tastefully done elegant theme. They both have a love for live theatre, so they rented out an entire theatre house.

As Jeremy and I enter through the main doors and into the lobby, my breath gets caught in my throat. The ceiling is so high, even if you were on the second story it is still so incredibly endlessly high. Walls are maintained with the original wallpaper that has the orange brown stain from when you were legally allowed to smoke in the theatres. I bet good money that if I went up to smell the wallpaper it would hold the light stench. A smell you would obviously miss if you weren't intentionally seeking it out.

As I continue to take in architecture of the building, I'm giddy over this for an entirely different reason than my cousin and her soon to be hubby are. My interest is the architecture as well and design; it's actually what I am majoring in at university. Majoring in architectural design with a minor in interior design.

The marble flooring and regal masculinity of the evening bar, just wow, maybe I should get into live theatre myself and have the full experience.

"Poppie, let's go check our coats with the attendant. The ceremony starts in less than ten minutes and we still need to find our way to the grand theatre hall plus seats." Jeremy grabs my attention from my inner drooling.

"This place… it's just…"

"It's your ooey gooey. I know and trust me, babe, you'll have time afterwards to admire the building. But missing even a moment of your cousin's wedding I know will upset you. So, no more getting distracted."

The way he says admire, dripping with playful sarcasm, but the joke is on him. Once this ceremony is over, he is going to be the one to have to deal with my endless commentary and the questions we both know I will ask the manager or anyone else who works here that will give me the time of day. Yes, I'm that bad. No, I don't care.

We make our way to the only theatre hall that isn't blocked off with the red rope linked to gold poles. With how expansive the hall is the balcony entrance is closed off so we cannot sit up there, but that makes sense because if anyone did, they wouldn't be able to see the bride and groom or hear anything that they are saying from where they are on the stage.

Once finding our seats, it hasn't been more than a few minutes before the music starts that indicates Lorall will start her walk down to the aisle. Taking a brief moment, I give my attention to Harrison. Hearing the door open I want to catch the look on his face seeing the love of his life in her wedding dress for the first time. His smile morphs into one of shock for less than ten seconds then morphs again to adoration. Some recognition went through his mind. I'll make sure to ask Harrison when he has a moment later today. Turning my attention back to my cousin she shares a knowing smile with Harrison, something only the two of them are aware of.

When she passes by me, she briefly reaches out and squeezes my hand and I give her hand one back. It only taking a moment as to not get them off track with the song.

Since I've found out what was in my file her and I have only seen each other in passing at work, but she knows about everything going down. Though we have been in contact over text and phone since my seeking help with Dr. Deigh, I am just so incredibly happy to share her special day with her.

"Good morning, everyone," the woman marrying them starts, captivating the audience from the first word spoken.

***

The whole wedding was an experience, by the time the service was over the lobby was set up to hold the reception. The center of the lobby was set to be the dance floor with the tables staggered around but also lining the makeshift dance floor area. With both the traditional newlywed dance then followed by the father daughter dance, which Lorall called people to join in on so I danced with my dad. While Dad and I danced, we made light chit chat on my wedding plans, smiling and laughing with each other. It warms my heart that Lorall and Harrison found each other.

Me being the nosey person I am talked Lorall into sharing the details of her and Harrison's honeymoon plans. Let me tell you, it was easy to break her resolve and once I did, she gushed, and we conversed like teen girls talking about their crushes. Her and Harrison are headed up to a resort up in the mountains where they plan on snowboarding and enjoying the snow. I told her she has to take lots of photos and make a snowman for me, which made her laugh and tell me she would see what she could do.

Now Jeremy and I are sat in our living room having barbeque pork mashed potatoes and corn for dinner. Before coming home after we left the reception, we stopped off at a store to get candy and all sorts of junk food. Our plan is to have a horror movie slash Halloween movie marathon. It's been my thing to do for Halloween since sixth grade no matter how hard my friends tried to get me to join them every year. I never deviated from my tradition and Jeremy has joined me since the first Halloween after we met. One night about a week before Halloween he asked me what my plans were and so I told him and for some reason decided to ask him if he wanted to join. I had never before asked anyone if they wanted to be a part of my tradition before but for some reason felt compelled to ask him. Now it's both of our tradition. Jeremy once even told me that he really loved that I wasn't the type to go out and party on Halloween; when he had told me that I saw the sincerity in his eyes and that he wasn't just making fun of me. Obviously, I was one that enjoyed a good party like any other teenage girl would but adding a day where you can disguise yourself as anything you can imagine and then adding alcohol, it simply always screamed recipe for disaster to me. Even with that thought that went through my mind every year when I turned down my friends, I always felt more comfortable in my skin doing my own thing. Almost as a small reprieve within myself, giving myself the permission to not fit a mold I wanted to fit.

With all the lights out, front door locked and a note on the door to let trick or treaters know that they won't get anything from this house, we are now ready to start our marathon uninterrupted.

"All righty let's get this madness started shall we." Jeremy takes the remote and presses play on the movie *Ghost Ship*.

Chapter Thirteen
Xena?

Mom and Dad called Jeremy and I over for lunch today. They said they have information for me about the case. I wonder what they have. I hope it's the location of the Mirth brothers and what their plan is to apprehend them. I still want justice for me and all the kids who suffered by their hands. Though, if I am being completely honest with myself, I'm just ready for this all to be over with. Thinking that maybe, maybe it's time to let this go so I can move on from it and heal. I hate myself for even having the thought and know that if the Mirth brothers don't get caught that the reality of them ever changing their line of work would be like me telling another survivor that what happened to them doesn't matter and that they don't deserve justice.

After meeting up with my parents today I should probably meet with Dr. Deigh. "Hello, you've reached Dr. Deigh's office, my name is Justine, how may I help you?"

"Yes, I need to make an emergency appointment with Dr. Deigh, do you have anything for this afternoon, if possible after two p.m.?"

"Let me see here, just one moment. From what I see here there are only two openings in her schedule today. The earliest time you can get in at is two thirty and the other time slot is at four p.m. Do either of those work for you?"

"Hmm, yah can I get the four p.m. slot. That would work the best for me."

"We can do that for you. Now, I'm sorry if I've already asked, but I don't remember asking for your name."

"Oh! I'm so sorry, yes my name is Poppie Raven."

"All right Miss Raven, the appointment has been scheduled for four p.m. And I'm sure you are aware of payment procedure, but we just need to make sure you have the payment method with you at time of arrival and that you will have to pay before you go to her office and meet with her. Okay?"

"That won't be a problem, thank you for getting me set up on such short notice."

"Not a problem, goodbye."

"Goodbye."

Once I end the call I'm startled by Jeremy as he clears his throat gaining my attention, causing me to tense and spin around and face him. "Shit, Jer, make a noise next time. I'm going to keel over from fright one of these times."

"Hey now, I was trying to be respectful to the fact that you were on a phone call. No attitude, missy. You ready to go have lunch with your parents?"

Walking up to him I embrace him in a hug and lay the side of my face to his chest, taking a moment to breathe him in. Hugs are my absolute favorite thing in the world, only a handful of people I've ever hugged have had the kind of hug that I seek. The kind where you feel the strength and security as well as the warmth and love the person has for you. Yah, that kind; and Jeremy has that kind of hug.

"As ready as one can be with the unknown journey we are on."

As we pull up out front of my parents' house, the anticipation of what Mom and Dad have to tell me makes me grow anxious as to whether or not that it's good or bad news. Looking out at their house I see my parents laughing with each other at whatever they are talking about. I can only assume that what they have to tell us can only be good news. I don't believe they'd be this uplifted if it were bad news; even if right now it's only them, bad news would keep them solemn with them knowing we are headed over to meet them.

Jeremy and I sit in the car for a few moments longer just observing them; the love you can see clearly written across their faces, even after all these years or the joy present with the calm of the early afternoon spending time together. Maybe in my own hopeful thoughts, them knowing that they will always be my parents, blood or not has no significance to me. The people who are there for you, making the choice to love you unconditionally, supporting you no matter what. That is the true definition of what a parent is and mine have all those qualities.

As we walk up, both Jeremy and I are greeted with warm hugs from both my parents. Once we've exchanged hugs with them both I walk over to Mom's spot at the table. I hijack her mug and drink the cinnamon hot cocoa inside, only cooled enough to not scald the tongue. *Perfect stolen goods. Jeez Poppie enter in a cackle and the curled smile of the old, animated Grinch and I've got myself the perfect criminal.* Internally I laugh at my personal thoughts. *So me.*

"Poppie Blithe, get your grubby paws off my yummy hot cocoa, young lady." Mom scoffs at me in fake anger. Like it's a surprise that I'm doing this when all present know this is something I do often enough for it to be of no surprise to them.

"So, Piper, Andrew, what's going on with the case? Good news, right?"

"Let's go inside to talk about it. It is most definitely good news, but it might take some moments of processing. Understandably so."

"Sure, Mom, but no more waiting, the buildup is killing us."

"Of course, hun."

With my stolen goods in hand, we head inside and take a seat in the living room; thankfully, Dad jumps right into it with Mom sitting next to him with a slight hopeful smile.

“We’ve found the girl who befriended you, Eighteen. Her legal name is Xena Keenan; through the F.B.I we brought her in and asked some standard questions that might help with the case. Also, because we knew you’d be okay with it we told her about you. Quite frankly she bawled her eyes out when she heard you were saved and would like the chance to meet up with you tomorrow. Do you think that would be something you’d like to do?”

“Dad, that… that would be absolutely amazing.”

“Good, because your father and I already said yes and set up a time and place. She seems like she adjusted back to normal life and didn’t let being exposed to the cruel incident stop her from living her life the way she desires.”

“I want to know how you guys tracked her down, but I acknowledge that it’s confidential and I don’t want to jeopardize your guys’ careers. Thank you so much, this is some of the best news since starting this whole journey.”

“Poppie, it’s absolutely incredible; babe, I am so excited for you to meet her. Would you want me to go with you? Actually, you know what, Xena might feel more comfortable talking to you without me present and I don’t want to interrupt any possibility of you two really talking with each other.”

Jeremy is such a compassionate person and in tune with true emotions. Not as a rude thought, but more so as a completely unbiased thought; if I didn’t know he was straight I would think he may be gay if not bi. I can guarantee that if he weren't straight, we'd still be inseparable only as best friends and not as a couple.

"I think you might be right, Jer, I don't want her to feel uncomfortable when we meet up. Dad what are the meet up details?"

"We've set you two up to meet at Terrebonne Po' Boys directly at noon. Also here is a picture of her so you know who to look out for."

"Thanks, Dad, Mom. I really appreciate this."

***

It's now time for my meeting with Dr. Deigh; after my parents let us know the surprising news, we still had a couple hours to spare considering that whole conversation took less than thirty minutes. We then had lunch like we planned on doing then played some card games to pass the time and hang out with each other. It was a good way to calm my ever-growing nerves for tomorrow as well helped put me in a good mind frame before meeting with Dr. Deigh.

"So what is today's emergency visit for? Are you okay? Mom and Dad doing okay? Jeremy and the wedding planning?"

"Yes, everything is going good actually, Mom and Dad had a break in the case and were able to track down Eighteen. You remember me telling you about her?"

She nods in silent agreement answering my question, motioning for me to continue.

"Well my parents found her, and while they were talking to her to see if she had any information that might help with their investigation, they mentioned me and set up a time and place for us to meet and talk. I'm extremely overjoyed that she was saved. I still loathe the fact that not all the kids were saved, but she befriended me and took me under her wing. I would be absolutely destroyed if she hadn't had been rescued."

"This seems like a pretty big breakthrough in the case. How are you feeling about seeing her after all these years? And if I may ask, what is her real name? I believe for her own justice even if she isn't here to hear our conversation, we should give her the respect of calling her by her name not what those men called her."

"Oh yes, her name is Xena Keenan, though that's all my parents told me about her. They don't want to give me any information about Xena because they don't want to invade her personal information without her knowledge or approval. Which I respect completely, it wouldn't be kind. And to answer your other question. Honestly, I don't know how I feel. I know I feel excitement and a good nervous energy is coursing through me. But am I allowed to feel that way, should I be more wary of it all. And how do I talk with her?"

"The best advice I can give you is to be open, open to her freely on your feelings and open to feeling her own feelings. What all you kids went through is nothing small; the strength that had to have taken for each kid to live through that. Well that's simply something only you and her can understand. I can only hope to understand and help. Would it help if you practiced some questions now? I could help you write some questions down that you want to ask her in case you freeze up."

"You know what, that sounds like a great idea, it might calm my mind some feeling somewhat prepared and not just leaving it up to chance or what not."

We write down a good handful of questions as well as a few conversation starters. She also suggested I dress in comfortable clothes, saying how being in uncomfortable clothes on top of an anxiety heightening situation makes for a hell of an uncomfortable idea all together. It's a good suggestion honestly and one that I'm going to take.

When our time comes to an end, I'm almost sad leaving, wishing we can have more time. Sometimes I forget that she is my therapist and not just a friend. Though, with the list of questions in my hand and a successful meeting with Dr. Deigh has given me a renewed sense of assurance.

Chapter Fourteen
Terrebonne Po' Boys

I arrive at Terrebonne Po' Boys about ten minutes early so I can secure us a table in this quaint little corner restaurant. As well I decided to be early so I could look out for her and hope that she isn't already here waiting for me.

Entering the building I briefly look around for her and finding that she indeed isn't here yet calms my nerves ever so slightly. Feeling the list of written down question folded up into my clammy fisted palm, I find a perfect spot for us. Sitting down I unfold the paper, trying to flatten it out. I skim over the questions once more rehearsing them in my mind. I'm not one who always has to feel in control, quite the opposite actually. I enjoy letting things fall as they may, putting just that extra dash of adventure in my life. Today however it's unsettling and I want some semblance of control.

I only get to run through my questions twice before I see Xena walking through the door. With a small smile I wave her over.

Xena is absolutely stunning, she is literally glowing. Caramel curly hair that looks to have a mind of its own, light blue almond shaped eyes, a button nose, her lips well rounded and symmetrical. I want to guess 5'7", warm honey colored skin impeccably smooth without a blemish in sight. Even her eyebrows are full but not bushy. She is even rocking a sunflower pattern long sleeve shirt with overall pants, and not the skinny jean kind but real ones, and red converse with the tops folded down. Topping off the look there are a pair of sunglasses in her wild hair.

“Poppie Raven? I’m Xena Keenan, though when we met, I was called Eighteen.”

“Wow, it’s so surreal meeting you again after all these years. It’s nice though.”

“I do agree with you on that; I’m overjoyed that you were saved that day. From what both Raven agents tell me not every kid was rescued.”

“Unfortunately so. When I found that out I was extremely upset with my parents. I couldn’t believe they didn’t save every kid; I even went into a downward spiral for gosh now I can’t remember but at least a week. It wasn’t good that’s for sure. Though the case has been reopened and I am trying to remember anything I can to help with the investigation.”

“I’m sorry if this may seem rude, but your parents don’t look anything like you. Are you adopted?”

“Hmm… Oh, yes, I am. It turned out that my biological parents didn’t want me, so I was left with my grandparents who turns out also didn’t want me and they sold me to some men who then tried to sell me to the Mirth brothers, but from what I can remember the

Mirth brothers killed those other men. I wasn't kidnapped. That memory there actually caused me to have nightmares since about that night. It spurred me on to figure out why I was having that nightmare, which turned out to be a memory not a nightmare at all. Back to my parents as I've gotten off on a tangent here. I love my parents though; they are my parents the other people were just how I came to be."

After a short moment of silence between the two of us, a question nags at the back of my mind causing me to speak again.

"Can I ask how your life has been? What happened to you afterwards?"

"When I was rescued some of the other agents who were a part of the case asked if I knew my name and how long I had been missing for. It was hard for me at first, I wouldn't talk for two days straight. I couldn't let myself believe it was all over; I had been missing for six years.

"Questions ran through my mind; were my parents still looking for me, would my parents assume that I had been dead all this time, how would I cope returning back to a normal life. I was fourteen by that point. Thoughts on high school and if I were even educated enough to start with my year or if I'd have to play catch up. I was resistant to the point that I started to drive myself crazy with thoughts of all the different possibilities.

"I don't know why no one ever bought me from the Mirth brothers, I did everything they wanted just so I could survive. To this day I still question why I never got bought. I'd like to think I had a guardian angel watching over me. My Noni passed on from a heart attack when I was kidnapped; it was right after my parents gave her the news. From what my parents say it literally broke her heart; her and I were really close when I was growing up. So I have a strong belief that she was protecting me all those years.

"I guess the agents became either desperate or determined because one day they took my picture and ran it through a software that had facial markers and it matched with one my parents gave all that time back when I went missing. So they got ahold of my parents. I don't exactly know what they had said to them, but less than twenty-four hours later I was face to face with my mom and dad. It was incredible, I just ran into their arms. The rest is an awfully long journey we all had to adjust to; a story for another time maybe."

I was stunned into silence throughout her whole recount; my heart ached for the girl sitting in front of me. Six years, and they never broke her, not fully. She may have complied with them to avoid punishment, but she is a survivor.

"Do… Do you by chance know my birth name? I cannot remember it for the life of me, and according to my adoption records no one was ever able to find out."

"Of course, one night we had confided in each other, hoping that someone would remember us. Your birth name is Dorrit Joyce Morningstar. Though from what you have told me about your birth parents, I would keep Poppie Raven. And whatever your middle name is, sorry your parents didn't tell me that."

"Oh, my middle name is Blithe, what about yours?"

"Mine is Ainsley. Xena Ainsley Keenan. Nice to meet you again, Poppie Blithe Raven."

"Likewise, Xena Ainsley Keenan."

Oddly enough we laugh and share stories about our lives. Eventually after the first bit we did make our food orders; by that point, our stomachs had settled, and we could enjoy the food without feeling like we might throw it back up just from nerves.

I don't know how long we've been sitting here for, but it must have been a substantial amount of time because another rush of people clamors in through the diner door. I do however vaguely remember us getting more drinks and some dessert during our time holding our current table hostage.

"Oh shit, sorry, Poppie, but my parents are blowing up my phone with texts. They insisted on accompanying me for the meeting with your parents as moral support and they have been keeping themselves busy while we've caught up. I really must go now though."

"I understand, my fiancé will want the whole scoop of today. He's been my rock through this whole endeavor. Could we swap numbers though and stay in contact?"

"Great minds think alike, I was just about to ask you the same question. Also, my parents and I are going to be in town for a few more days. I want to meet this fiancé of yours."

"Of course! Text me in the morning and maybe we can have lunch or dinner. You'll come to find I LOVE food."

With a humor filled laugh she agrees to what I've proposed. Once I've left a tip of about twenty percent of what I've spent today, we leave the diner heading to our separate cars. I'm assuming she had rented a car while over here.

While I drive back to Jeremy's and my place there is so much good adrenaline coursing through my veins for me to concentrate on one thought too long. Today went by so quickly as I check the clock on my dashboard; it says it's already six twenty in the evening. Arriving back home, with my car turned off, I take a moment closing my eyes and rest my head gently on my steering wheel taking in a few deep calming breaths before heading inside.

Stepping out of my car I notice the mugginess of the weather, silently thanking the Lord that I'm headed into an air-conditioned house. Before I can make it all the way to the door, Jeremy is already opening it for me to come in. With a soft smile on his handsome uneven lips, his arms are held open sending me an invitation that I simply cannot refuse nor one that I'd want to refuse. I'll never refuse a hug from him. It may sound cheesy, cliché, or even gag you sappy but I feel in my soul that if I did ever not hug him when given the chance it would damage my soul.

As we hug, all the tension leaves my body, but with that my emotions see an opening to take charge. Finding myself crying in his arms; crying over the fact that me and many other kids were put through what we were put through, crying for the thankfulness that I was rescued and so was Xena, crying in pain for those who were never saved, crying over the fact that I have a family that chose me and love me unconditionally when the ones who were supposed to never did. Tears of joy even flowed at the fact that the man I love loves me back and we are currently in the progress of getting wedding details done; ensuring that we want no one else in this world but each other for the rest of our lives.

I believe Jeremy knows what caused my breakdown, but even if he doesn't, he is doing exactly what I need in this moment. Jeremy is letting me experience all of these emotions without pushing me to say anything to him.

"Mark this day, Jer, November second; I finally feel like I have gotten the closure I need."

Jeremy is stunned into stillness by my comment and I can see the gears turning in his head of the possible questions he might have for me. I just patiently wait for him to compose himself enough to ask me what ever question he has.

"Poppie, I don't think I understand fully what you are saying. Wha… how… hmph."

Not seeming to get his thoughts out like he would like, I decide to spare him and further explain myself. "I still I am going to help my parents with whatever I can on their investigation and If I'm lucky enough I do want to at least have a conversation with Twenty, Austin, ugh whatever his name may be. I think speaking with him might give me a different kind of closure than meeting Xena did. We are all survivors it's simply different methods of surviving that we have all had to adjust to. However, I am ready to not let this run my life any longer. With just the thought that my parents have reopened the case and that I am at their disposal to help out is enough for me. Now I get to fully focus on our wedding and with sticking with therapy will help with my emotions and any other memories I remember in the future."

Love and respect is all I see on Jeremy's face and for that I'm eternally grateful. He will always be my partner in crime.

"Well soon-to-be-Mrs. Ross, you've got my one hundred percent support. Plus we are more than halfway done with wedding planning. So that's a definite bonus."

"Mark the day, Jer, because I know we were already in the stages of planning the wedding, but now no emotional stings are affecting me, and I want to set a date. I want to be married in a month from now."

"December second?"

"December second."

www.ingramcontent.com/pod-product-compliance
Ingram Content Group UK Ltd.
Pitfield, Milton Keynes, MK11 3LW, UK
UKHW040004200726
13854UKWH00001B/23

9 781800 161504